Praise for Adventures on Trains

'A thrilling and highly entertaining adventure story' David Walliams

'Wildly funny, with hairpin plot bends and inventive characters, this series is firmly on track to become a bestseller' *Daily Mail*

'Like *Murder on the Orient Express* but better. A terrific read!' Frank Cottrell-Boyce

'I have a station announcement: [M. G. Leonard and Sam Sedgman's] collaboration is a chuffing triumph!' *The Times* Children's Book of the Week

'Mysteries on trains . . . what' _____ 'ead in your life' Ross Montgomer _____ *ns*

'A pacey and intensely satis _____ ling golden age crime fiction sensib _____ ing' *Guardian*

'A super-fun middle-grade mystery' Peter Bunzl, author of *Cogheart*

'Ideal for _____ A _____ 10/21 _____ -fashioned mystery' _____

LB of Hackney

First published 2021 by Macmillan Children's Books
a division of Macmillan Publishers Limited
The Smithson, 6 Briset Street, London EC1M 5NR
EU representative: Macmillan Publishers Ireland Ltd, 1st Floor,
The Liffey Trust Centre, 117–126 Sheriff Street Upper
Dublin 1, D01 YC43
Associated companies throughout the world
www.panmacmillan.com

ISBN 978-1-5290-1312-2

1 3 5 7 9 8 6 4 2

A CIP catalogue record for this book is available from the British Library.

Printed and bound by CPI Group (UK) Ltd, Croydon CR0 4YY

M. G. LEONARD & SAM SEDGMAN

DANGER AT DEAD MAN'S PASS

Illustrated by *Elisa Paganelli*

MACMILLAN CHILDREN'S BOOKS

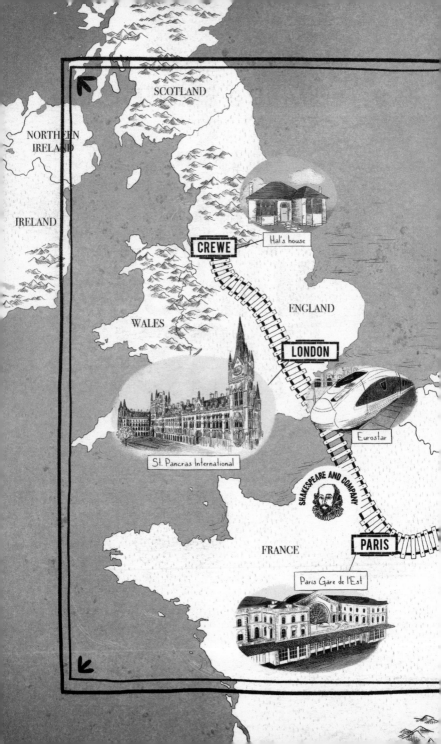

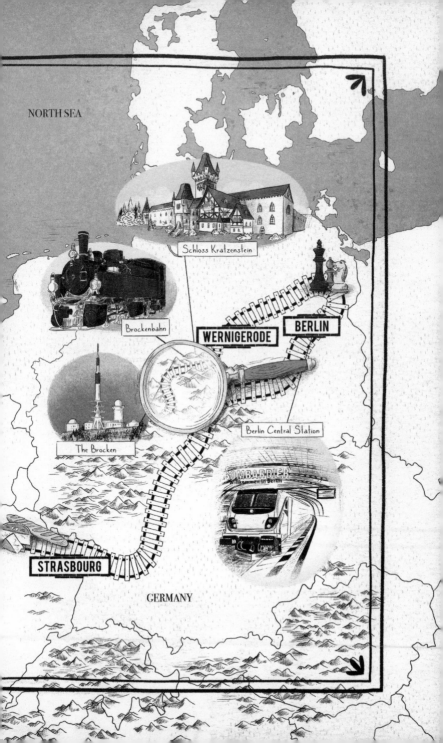

NORTH SEA

Schloss Kratzenstein

Brockenbahn

WERNIGERODE

BERLIN

The Brocken

Berlin Central Station

BOMBARDIER
Willkommen in Berlin

STRASBOURG

GERMANY

For my husband, Sam.

N U₂AHO FAC₂ UTR T₂EO UN₂ULNTk
MAC₂WTOF E₂O UWO AT T₂AKOT₂EOW

M. G. Leonard

For Bob, Kim and Rois.

E₂EA KUHO N₂O U IAWT₂ NT T₂EO I₂T₂AWN₂

Sam Sedgman

'Up Brocken mountain witches fly,

When stubble is yellow and green the crop.

Gathering on Walpurgis night,

Carrying Lucifer aloft.

Over stream and fern, gorse and ditch,

Tramp stinking goat and farting witch.'

Johann Wolfgang von Goethe,
Faust, Part I (lines 3956–61)

CHAPTER ONE

A LETTER ARRIVES

Hal and Ben were the last boys to leave the changing room after football practice. The school team trained in all weathers and, though the relentless rain of the past few days had finally stopped that afternoon, the pitch had been waterlogged and muddy. The freezing March wind had whipped at their bare legs and turned their fingers to icicles. It was so cold that Hal's misty breath had hidden the ball from him. Frostbitten and bruised from a match of sliding tackles, the boys had not been keen to go back outside. They dawdled in the warmth, rehashing the match and teasing each other, until they realized they were alone and it was getting late.

'We should go,' Hal said. 'Mum'll worry if I'm not home soon.' He picked up his bag.

As they walked away from the school building, Ben grabbed Hal's arm to halt him. 'Who's that?' he whispered, pointing through the gloom at the dark silhouette of a man, just beyond the school gates, cloaked in fog, waiting.

Hal caught his breath. He immediately recognized the tall figure in the dark peacoat. He'd drawn countless pictures of him. 'Uncle Nat!' he cried, bursting into a sprint, running to the gates. 'What are you doing here?'

'I've come to see you.' Nathaniel Bradshaw opened his arms wide and hugged his nephew.

'You're Hal's uncle?' Ben studied him with interest. 'The travel-journalist one that takes him on the train adventures?'

'He is.' Hal smiled proudly. 'Uncle Nat, this is Ben. Remember, I told you about him.'

'Yes. You're the young man with a soft spot for Sierra Knight, the movie star.'

Simultaneously delighted Uncle Nat knew who he was but embarrassed by his crush on the actress, Ben's mouth opened but no words came out.

'I didn't think you were coming till Easter Sunday,' Hal said, curious to know why his uncle was here more than a week early.

'A letter arrived for us this morning,' Uncle Nat said lightly, his voice contradicting his sombre expression as he withdrew an envelope from his coat and handed it to Hal. 'An old friend needs our help.'

'Are you taking Hal away on another adventure, Mr Bradshaw?' Ben asked.

'That depends on what you call an adventure.'

Schloss Kratzenstein
Wernigerode
Saxony-Anhalt
Germany

Nathaniel Bradshaw
The Old Rectory
Lincolnshire
England

23 March

Lieber Nathaniel,

How are you? Well, I hope?

A strange and unsettling matter provokes me to write to you with an unusual request.

Not knowing whom I can trust, I am asking you and your nephew Harrison for help. The matter concerns my wife Alma's side of the family, the Kratzensteins, whose business in railway construction and locomotive manufacture has made them wealthy, powerful and controversial. Three days ago, Alexander Kratzenstein, my wife's cousin, died suddenly at their family home in the Harz mountains.

Growing talk of an old family curse has been stoked by inexplicable events surrounding Alexander's death. The doctor assures us his death was natural, a heart attack, but I have seen the expression on his face.

It was twisted with terror. I believe he died of fright. A ghostly figure has been seen on the mountain. And early this morning, Alma's uncle swears he saw a witch standing on Dead Man's Pass: the stretch of railway line beyond the house.

My little mouse, Alma, is scared for the lives of our children, Oliver and (your friend) Milo, as the curse is said to fall on the sons of Kratzensteins. I am not one to believe in old superstitions, but something sinister is happening here at Schloss Kratzenstein. After a thorough search, it seems that Alexander's will is missing.

As the funeral is to be held next Monday, I am hoping to persuade you and Harrison to attend disguised as distant relatives. I want you to do what you do best: investigate these strange occurrences and discover the truth behind them.

Naturally, you have questions. I enclose two tickets for the Eurostar from London St Pancras and invite you to have lunch with me in Paris, at Le Train Bleu in Gare de Lyon, tomorrow, when I will answer them. Bring an overnight bag for onward travel to Berlin, and speak of this to no one.

Mit herzlichen Grüßen,

Baron Wolfgang Essenbach

'Tomorrow?' Hal looked up.

'Yes. We'll have to catch the London train.' Uncle Nat pulled up his sleeve and looked at one of the three wrist watches strapped to it. 'In an hour and nine minutes, to be precise.'

'It's true,' Ben whispered. 'You do wear six watches.'

'Bev told me today was the last day of school before the Easter holiday.'

'Mum's going to let me go with you?' Hal was surprised. His mum had been very upset when she'd heard there'd been a murder on their last train journey.

'She's not happy, but I argued that we had nothing to do with the theft, the kidnapping or the murder on our previous journeys.' He smiled ruefully. 'Other people's wrongdoings shouldn't stop you from seeing the world.'

'Did you show her the letter?'

Uncle Nat pushed his tortoiseshell glasses up his nose, glancing at Ben who was listening with wide eyes. He chose his words carefully as he replied, 'I told her that the baron's an old friend of ours who has invited us to go to Germany, and has a wonderful model railway that you'd love to see. Bev said as long as I get you back before Easter, and there were no murders on our trip, you could come. She's packing your rucksack right now.'

'She is?' Hal felt an uncomfortable prickle in his chest. He didn't like keeping things from his mum.

'Hal,' Uncle Nat said softly, 'in all the years that I've known the baron, he's never once asked for my help. I . . . I thought you might want to come, at least to Paris. But if you'd rather not I would understand, and I'm sure the baron would too.'

Ben looked from Uncle Nat to Hal.

Hal stared down at the letter in his hands. A puzzling death. A curse. A missing will. Adopting a disguise. He could feel his heart beating. He handed back the letter. He'd made up his mind. 'Of course I want to come.'

'Has there been a crime?' Ben asked, so curious he looked like he might burst.

'No, not a crime. A mystery,' Uncle Nat replied.

'And we are going to solve it.' Hal looked at his uncle. 'Right?'

'Right,' Uncle Nat agreed.

'I wish I could come,' Ben said.

'You can be our man on the ground, Ben,' Uncle Nat said.

'Really? Great! What do I do?'

'Act like everything is normal and don't breathe a word of our conversation to anyone,' Uncle Nat said, gravely.

'I can do that. You can trust me.'

Hal laughed. 'I'll tell you everything when I get back,' he promised.

'You'd better.'

'We have to go.' Uncle Nat put a hand on Hal's shoulder. 'We've not got much time. We have to make that train. Let's go get your things and say goodbye to your mum.' He looked from Hal to Ben, and back at Hal. 'Remember, this is a trip to see an old friend's model railway, nothing more.'

'Got it,' Hal and Ben replied in unison.

CHAPTER TWO

WANDERLUST

When he got home, Hal had just enough time to change his clothes, hang his silver train whistle round his neck, grab his rucksack, hug his dog, Bailey, and kiss his mum and little sister goodbye before the taxi arrived. He and Uncle Nat hurried into Crewe station, through the barriers, over the footbridge and on to the platform for the London train.

'Here's your ticket.' Uncle Nat thrust the orange card at Hal as a line of green-and-white carriages, stuffed with people, pulled up alongside them. 'I was too late to reserve seats. Let's hope we can find two together.'

The carriage doors beeped and opened, releasing a torrent of people who pushed past, barely glancing at them. Hal spotted a pair of empty seats and they dropped into them, putting their bags at their feet.

'According to the timetable, we arrive in Euston just before 7.30 p.m.,' Uncle Nat said, unbuttoning his coat. 'It's a short walk from there to King's Cross. I've booked us a twin room in the St Pancras Renaissance Hotel, which is directly above the station. In the morning, it'll be a two-minute walk from breakfast to the Eurostar terminal.'

A thrill rocketed up Hal's spine. Today had started off like any normal school day, walking to school with Ben, but now he was on a train to London with his favourite uncle, and they were travelling to Paris, to help Baron Essenbach with a strange death and a family curse! The platform of Crewe station slid from view, and the electric light in the carriage turned the window into a mirror, showing Hal his grinning reflection. This time he had a case to solve before he'd even got on a train.

Lowering the plastic seat-table, he pulled a small pocketbook and black art pen from his coat pocket. He'd wanted to bring a sketchbook and pencil case, because it was through drawing that he unravelled mysteries, but Uncle Nat had pointed out that the baron had asked them to disguise themselves. A few newspapers had printed stories about the cases Hal had solved, describing him as 'the Drawing Detective', and Uncle Nat was concerned that artist's materials might blow his cover. And so Hal had brought only a pocketbook and a couple of art pens.

Pulling the lid off one, Hal drew his school gates and, beyond them, Uncle Nat shrouded in fog. His heart lifted as he shaded the mist with a light cross-hatch pattern. Another adventure was beginning. He could feel it.

'The baron has booked us on the earliest Eurostar tomorrow. It leaves St Pancras at 7.55 a.m. and gets into Paris Gare du Nord at 11.17, giving us plenty of time to hop on the Métro and meet him for lunch in Le Train Bleu.'

'Do you speak French?' Hal asked, noticing how easily the foreign words rolled off his uncle's tongue.

'I flatter myself that I could pass for French if I spent a month or two there,' Uncle Nat replied. 'How about you?'

'*Je ne parle pas français*,' Hal said haltingly.

'Ha! Well, there's no better way to learn a language than to be surrounded by it. Perhaps you can impress your mum with a few German phrases when you get home. If Bev believes this trip has been educational, she might forgive our investigative escapades.'

'I don't speak any German,' Hal confessed. 'Apart from I know that the German for father is *farter*.'

'It's *Vater*!' Uncle Nat laughed. 'I read German better than I speak it, but it's a fabulous language. Many words sound like English. One of my favourite German words is *Wanderlust*. It means the desire to travel.'

'Wanderlust,' Hal repeated, thinking of the journey they were embarking upon. 'Can I look at the letter again? I should read it properly before we meet the baron.'

Uncle Nat hesitated, then took it from the inside pocket of his coat and passed it over.

'Are you and the baron good friends?' Hal asked, unfolding the paper.

'I suppose so. We move in the same circles.' Hal noticed his uncle's cheerful tone contradicted the tension he could see in the man's jawline and forehead. He realized with surprise that Uncle Nat was worried about something. 'Our shared passion for trains means we often bump into each other, on the Highland Falcon, for example. I once dined at his castle and he showed me his marvellous model railway. He's fine company and I like him enormously, but he is a great and important man. I'm not sure I'd dare say he was my friend.'

'But he must think of you as his friend, or why would he write to you?'

'I suppose he must do.'

'What do you think about the Kratzenstein curse?'

'I don't believe in curses.' Uncle Nat frowned. 'They prey on people's fears. Often they are used as a cover by someone who's up to no good.'

'Do you think a member of the Kratzenstein family is up to no good? That they're responsible for Alexander's death?' Hal lowered his voice to a whisper. 'Do you think it could be *murder?*'

'The doctor said he died of a heart attack, but, like you, I only know what's in that letter.'

'I wonder what Dead Man's Pass is? The ghostly witch sounds spooky.' Hal shuddered with a sudden thrill.

'One step at a time. Let's get to Paris and hear what the baron has to say first. I'd like to be sure of what we're getting ourselves into before we agree to sneak into a family's house pretending to be people we're not and attending a funeral for a man we've not met.' Uncle Nat turned away, looking out of the window, indicating the conversation was over.

*

Euston station reminded Hal of an underground car park, all diesel-stained concrete and brightly coloured signs. He followed Uncle Nat up a gentle ramp on to the main concourse, where they were confronted by a wall of people with luggage, staring up at information boards. A platform was announced, and a crowd of passengers grabbed their wheely suitcases and charged towards their train like a pack of herded animals.

'Keep close,' Uncle Nat called out.

Outside, the night sky was black and the pavement sparkled with reflected city lights, twinkling in the puddles.

'Our hotel is in that direction,' Uncle Nat indicated, and they hurried away from the station with their heads down, walking into the wind. Barely five minutes later, he announced, 'That's the hotel up ahead.'

Hal's mouth dropped open as they approached an enormous Victorian redbrick building with an impressive Gothic facade, hundreds of windows and a clock tower. 'It looks like the Houses of Parliament!'

'Once, it was offices for British Rail, but now it's a rather smart hotel. I told your mother to pack your swimming things because there's a pool in the old underground kitchens. I thought you might like a dip before dinner.' Uncle Nat smiled at the expression on Hal's face. 'Come on, let's check in.'

CHAPTER THREE

THE EUROSTAR

Hal woke up before the alarm. He crept from his bed and peered out of the window at the sun rising above the red walls of the British Library. He was wide awake and eager to start the day. Going into the bathroom, he splashed water on his face, and pulled on his clothes, stuffing his pyjamas into his rucksack. When he came out, Uncle Nat was up and getting dressed. Ten minutes later they were both packed and on their way down to breakfast.

Hal wolfed down a bowl of cereal and necked a glass of orange juice. Uncle Nat didn't eat. He drank two coffees, made certain he had their passports and tickets, then went to check out of the hotel. When Hal joined him beside the reception desk, the woman behind it was handing over a large brown envelope.

'What's that?' Hal asked as they made their way into the station.

'Yesterday, when I got the baron's letter, I rang the *Telegraph* travel desk and asked my editor to pull together

14

some information for us about the Kratzenstein family.' He waved the envelope. 'We can read it on the train.'

St Pancras International was a grand old station and yet felt modern. The classic brick arches housed posh boutiques and cafes, and the vaulted steel roof held panes of polished glass. Hal could hear somebody playing a piano as they approached the Eurostar check-in desk, signposted in royal blue. Within minutes, their passports had been scanned, their bags rolled through a security scanner and they were standing in the departure lounge.

'It's quicker than an airport,' Hal remarked as they sat down opposite a sign reminding them to change their pounds into euros.

'More civilized,' Uncle Nat agreed. 'And though planes travel faster than trains, they can't drop you in the heart of a city.'

When boarding was announced, they joined a queue of people shuffling up a travelator to the platform. Hal anticipated the acrid stink of diesel, but above the blue-and-grey carriages striped with yellow, he spied wires and realized the Eurostar was electric. Stepping off the travelator, he dodged round a woman struggling with a giant suitcase.

Hal whistled, leaning to one side so he could see the engine. 'That is a long train.'

'It's a quarter of a mile long,' Uncle Nat agreed. 'The engineers use bicycles to get from one end to the other. Shall we go and say hello to the loco?'

The pair hurried along the platform, grinning, excited

to see the face of the electric engine that would take them through the Channel Tunnel, under the sea, to France.

The Eurostar nose was long like a greyhound's. It had a sunny yellow face with a dove-grey chin and a dark blue slipstreamed body. It looked light, fast and more friendly than the colossal diesels that had pulled the California Comet.

'An e320,' said Uncle Nat approvingly. 'The newest rolling stock. The 320 refers to kilometres per hour, their top speed. There's an engine at both ends of the train, in case we get stuck in the tunnel.'

'Has that ever happened?' Hal had his pocketbook and pen out and was drawing the engine's face.

'Yes, but it's rare and usually due to extreme weather conditions.'

Hal sketched in the windscreen, and noticed the train driver was watching him. He waved. The driver smiled and waved back.

Once he'd finished his sketch, they retraced their steps back down the platform.

'Here's our carriage,' said Uncle Nat.

'It's First Class!' Hal gasped.

'Business Premier,' Uncle Nat corrected him as they climbed aboard. 'The baron doesn't travel any other way.' He pointed at a pair of single seats facing each other over a table. 'That's us.'

Hal sat down and stared at the glass meeting cubicles in the centre of the room. It was the most office-like carriage he'd ever seen. After a while, an announcer welcomed them aboard the Eurostar in English and then in French. The doors closed and Hal felt the gentle lurch of the train moving out of St Pancras station accompanied by the low humming sound of the electric engine. He looked out across London. The early morning sun sliced through the low ashen clouds with swords of lemon light, and the palette of industrial greys was spattered with a lime-green suggestion of spring. It was hard to believe that in less than three hours he'd be in Paris. It had taken that long to get here from Crewe.

'Shall we find out what's in here?' Uncle Nat pulled out the brown envelope he'd been given in the hotel and placed it on the table between them. From it, he slid a wad of paper. 'The Kratzenstein family's business, K-Bahn, builds railways and sells rolling stock. After the Second World War, Arnold

17

Kratzenstein inherited the company and ran it for years. He's still alive at the grand old age of eighty-two. Alexander Kratzenstein, was his eldest son. He took over the business seventeen years ago.'

Hal pulled out his pocketbook and, turning to a double blank page, began to draw a family tree. He needed a way to remember who everyone was, and he knew a picture would work best. He put Arnold at the top. 'Alexander is the one who has died?'

'Yes.' Uncle Nat pulled a copy of a newspaper article from the wad of papers. 'Look, his obituary was printed yesterday. This will be helpful.'

'Can I see?'

'It's written in German.' Uncle Nat showed him the page and Hal's heart sank. How was he going to do any detecting if he couldn't understand what anyone was saying or had written down? 'It says that Alexander is survived by his wife, Clara – an artist – and their son, Herman, aged nine.'

Hal wrote these names on the family tree and drew a railway line from Alexander's name to his wife's and his son's.

'Interesting. Alexander has an older son from a previous marriage. He's nineteen and named Arnold, after his grandfather.'

Hal added him to the family tree too.

'I wonder who will run the family business now?' Furrows of concentration appeared on Uncle Nat's forehead as he shuffled through the pages.

An attendant arrived with a trolley and laid out two trays

on their table containing pastries, tiny pots of jam, a yogurt, and a hot dish covered with foil.

'Could I trouble you for a coffee?' Uncle Nat asked the attendant, who duly poured one.

'Who is Alma Essenbach's uncle?' Hal asked. 'In his letter, the baron said that Alma's uncle saw a witch on Dead Man's Pass, and that the Kratzensteins were her family.'

'Alma's in her late fifties, so I would imagine it must be old Arnold Kratzenstein. That would mean that either her mother or father is Arnold's sister or brother.'

Hal drew in a new branch of the family tree, adjoined to Arnold, and below it he marked in Alma. As he did so, Uncle Nat pushed his food aside. 'Aren't you eating?'

'I'm not hungry.'

'Is everything OK?' Hal could see something was bothering him.

'If I'm honest, I'm worried about what we're getting mixed up in.'

'But the baron wouldn't put us in danger,' Hal said, pushing his tray aside in solidarity.

'I know.' Uncle Nat smiled weakly and slid the papers back into the brown envelope. 'Oh, look, we're approaching the Channel Tunnel. You can tell by the fences.'

Through the window, Hal saw tall metal fence panels flying past, then suddenly the morning dissolved into darkness, strip lights on the ceiling lit up the carriage and the windows were black. As the train travelled deeper underground, Hal's hearing dimmed until his ears popped. He looked up at the ceiling, picturing a sea full of fish above them and boats sailing on its waters. 'How long will it take to reach France?'

'Usually, no more than half an hour. It's a thirty-mile stretch and the longest tunnel underneath the sea in the world.' Uncle Nat smiled. 'This tunnel is the most expensive engineering project ever undertaken.'

'It's cool,' Hal replied, more than a little awestruck.

Having grown accustomed to the darkness, Hal was blinded when the train finally burst out of the tunnel. 'We're in France!' he said, half standing in his seat to look out of the window, but to his surprise France looked a lot like England. The weather was drab; a thin fog lingered over the bare treetops as they sped past wide flat fields and electricity pylons. As the train accelerated, Hal's view became blurred, and he felt pinned to his seat as if they were about to make the jump into hyperspace. He realized with glee that this was the fastest train he'd ever been on.

As they approached the outskirts of Paris, the Eurostar slowed down and the announcer spoke in French, then English, informing passengers they would soon be arriving at Gare du Nord.

'*Gare* means station,' Uncle Nat said, 'and *Nord* is north.'

'*Gare du Nord*,' Hal repeated. 'Station of the North?'

'It's the station for trains going north of Paris.'

The doors hissed open. Hal felt a lurch as he stepped down on to the platform of Gare du Nord and heard a passing couple speaking French. He moved closer to Uncle Nat. The station was beautiful: columns of mint-green ironwork stretched up to high arched windows. He couldn't understand the French signs, but saw English words underneath the French.

'This way to the Métro.' Uncle Nat led him to an escalator that took them down into a hall lined with shops. They approached a wall of ticket machines and Hal watched with interest as Uncle Nat's fingers danced over the touchscreen.

'*Voila, ton billet,*' he said, passing Hal a white strip of card, 'means "your ticket".' He smiled. 'We take the RER line D two stops south, to Gare de Lyon.'

'*Gare de Lyon,*' Hal said, trying to sound French. 'Station for trains to Lyon?'

'Yes!' Uncle Nat looked pleased. 'And lunch with the baron!'

CHAPTER FOUR

LE TRAIN BLEU

U ncle Nat and Hal squeezed on to the crowded Métro train. There was an abrupt honking sound and the doors snapped shut with a startling *bang*. Above the door was a map with tiny lights that lit up as the train visited each station on the route. It was only two stops to Gare de Lyon, and Hal was relieved when it was their turn to get off, and rise up the escalators. He wondered what sort of place Le Train Bleu was, and guessed it would be posh.

'Is the restaurant on a train?' he asked Uncle Nat as they emerged in the bustling station.

'No, but it's named after a famous luxury sleeper train that travelled to the French Riviera. The restaurant was built in 1900, for the Exposition Universelle – a Parisian celebration of inventions in the city.' He led Hal to a sweeping stone staircase with a glazed archway at the top and *Le Train Bleu* spelt out in elegant white letters on a gold background.

'It's more than a hundred years old?' Hal marvelled.

'Yes, and every inch of the walls and ceiling are covered

in magnificent paintings, carvings and statues. I think you're going to like it.'

As they approached, the towering wooden doors opened and a man in a blue uniform welcomed them in. '*Bonjour, Messieurs, bienvenue au Train Bleu.*'

Inside, Hal found himself in the fanciest restaurant he'd ever seen. It looked like a palace. The high ceiling was painted like a cathedral with sumptuous murals, scenes of fun and joy in warm pastel colours, edged with gold.

'*Nous rencontrons un ami pour le déjeuner*, Baron Essenbach,' Uncle Nat said to a woman standing behind a counter. She picked up two menus and marched down the blue-carpeted aisle of the astonishingly cavernous restaurant. Hal tripped over his own feet while looking up at the gold chandeliers, each lightbulb a stamen nestled in a glistening flower.

Rows of neatly laid tables butted up to long wooden banquettes upholstered in blue leather and topped with brass luggage racks, giving the feel of a luxury dining car on a train.

The baron was sitting at a table beside an arch framed with gold winged cupids. He jumped to his feet when he saw them approaching. Dressed in an emerald waistcoat over a smoke-grey shirt, topped with a mustard cravat, his presence was impressive, but Hal noticed the bags under his eyes. The baron wore a worried expression that deepened the lines across his distinguished forehead.

'Nathaniel.' He shook their hands vigorously. 'Harrison. I cannot thank you enough for coming.'

'Of course,' Uncle Nat replied as he and Hal slid on to

the banquette, sitting opposite him.

'Let's order the food first, so we can talk.' The baron took the menus from the maître d, and she gestured to a waiter.

Hal stared at the list of French food on the menu. He didn't know what anything was. He spotted the word steak and was almost certain *pomme* was potatoes. He remembered in his French class they'd learned frites was chips. 'I'll have *steak tartare et pomme frites, s'il vous plait*, he told the waiter, hoping he was pronouncing it right.

'Are you sure?' Uncle Nat asked.

Hal nodded and handed back the menu. You couldn't go wrong with steak and chips.

Once the waiter had gone, the baron leaned forward, propping his elbows on the table, toying with his moustache as he looked over his shoulder to check no one was listening. 'I reserved the tables around us, so we don't have to whisper,' he said in a conspiratorial voice, and Hal felt the hairs on the back of his neck rise.

'We read the letter,' Hal said.

The baron gave Uncle Nat a look laden with meaning, and Uncle Nat gave an almost indiscernible dip of his head.

'Good, you must tell me what you make of the strange things that have happened.' He sat back in his chair and Hal took out his pocketbook and pen. 'Five days ago, my wife's cousin, Alexander Kratzenstein, was visiting his family home in Wernigerode. He went for a walk along the railway line beside the house and was found by Bertha, lying on the tracks in Dead Man's Pass, his face twisted in the most horrible grimace. He was dead.'

'Who is Bertha? Hal asked.

'Alexander's first wife.'

'And what is Dead Man's Pass?' Hal said, adding Bertha to the Kratzenstein family tree.

'A narrow-gauge steam railway runs from the town of Wernigerode to the peak of the Brocken mountain,' the baron explained. 'The Kratzensteins were involved in its construction in the late 1800s. A spur curves off the main line and leads to their house.

'They have their own train?'

'But of course – they are in the business of making trains.' The baron laughed at the expression on Hal's face.

'And Alexander Kratzenstein died in Dead Man's Pass?' Uncle Nat asked, and the baron nodded sombrely.

'Yes. Bertha called Alma with the terrible news. She still lives in Schloss Kratzenstein with Alexander's eldest son, Arnie.'

'Why is it called Dead Man's Pass?' Hal asked.

'I'm not certain. I think there was an accident there when the railway was being built.' The baron turned back to Uncle Nat. 'I left for the Harz mountains on Sunday, at Alma's request. Old Arnold is eighty-two and uses a wheelchair. Bertha has employed a nurse to take care of him, and adopted the duties of the housekeeper, but, apart from Arnie, the only other person in the house is Aksel, the groundsman.'

Hal made note of the groundsman and the nurse at the

25

bottom of the page. He would be checking they both had alibis.

'If Bertha, Alexander's first wife, lives in the family home,' Uncle Nat said, 'where are Clara and Herman Kratzenstein?'

'Berlin, which is where Alexander lived most of the time. He was visiting his father on business when he died.' He paused as a pair of waiters approached the table with a line of plates balanced on their arms, and gracefully deposited everybody's food and drinks.

'*Bon appétit*,' Uncle Nat said as they all picked up their cutlery.

Hal stared in horror at the plate put down in front of him. On it was a patty of uncooked minced beef with a raw egg yolk on top. 'I ordered steak,' he exclaimed.

'That is steak tartare,' Uncle Nat said, trying not to smile.

'But it's raw!'

'If you don't want it –' the baron moved the plate to his side of the table, chuckling – 'I am happy to eat it.'

'Do you want to order something else?' Uncle Nat asked.

'I'm fine with the chips,' Hal replied, relieved that at least he'd got that right.

'Traditionally, the family inters its deceased in the Kratzenstein crypt near the summit of the Brocken,' said the baron between mouthfuls. 'When I arrived at the house the next day, poor Alexander was laid out in the library.' He shook his head and muttered, '*Grässlich*.' He drew in a breath, then went on. 'The doctor, whom I met the next day, said Alexander died of a heart attack. I asked about the expression on his face,

26

but the doctor had no idea what might have caused it.'

'Strange,' Uncle Nat said.

'Indeed, and later that day, the family lawyer came to take Alexander's will from the safe, but it wasn't there.'

'Could it be in Berlin?' Uncle Nat asked.

The baron shook his head. 'The lawyer was confounded because Alexander had come to him the previous year to write a new will, and all the family's documents are kept in that safe. Nothing else was missing – only Alexander's will.'

'Do you think someone took it?' Hal asked.

'I don't know.' The baron pursed his lips and his moustache bristled. 'Alma believes it is the curse.'

'What is this curse?' Uncle Nat said, sceptically.

'The story is that hundreds of years ago a crazy witch cursed the family so that all the Kratzenstein men would meet a premature, and unnatural end.' The baron raised an eyebrow. 'Alma can list every Kratzenstein who died this way including Alexander's brother, Manfred, who died young, fighting with the French Foreign Legion.'

'Do you believe in the curse?' Hal asked, adding Manfred to the family tree beside Alexander, and writing *dead* next to his name.

'I do not believe in curses or the supernatural,' the baron replied. 'The mystery of what happened to Alexander is troubling. That is why I wrote to you. I want you to discover what happened in Dead Man's Pass that led to his heart attack. I can hardly investigate – it would be obvious what I was doing, and I must take care of the funeral.' He looked at Uncle

Nat, and there was a long moment of silence between the two men that baffled Hal.

'You polished of those chips quickly,' Uncle Nat said, turning to Hal. 'Your fingers are all greasy. Why don't you find the bathroom and wash your hands?'

It was more of an order than a suggestion, and Hal stood up, nodding, but he couldn't help feeling that something was going on that he was being kept out of. He slid his book and pen into his pocket and smiled brightly as he walked away from the table. Pausing a row of tables away, he glanced over his shoulder and saw Uncle Nat's concerned face leaning towards the baron. He dropped to the floor, wiping his hands on his jeans and pulling out his pocketbook. As he drew the scene, he listened intently, trying to catch what they were talking about.

'. . . never been triggered, not in all my professional career . . .' Uncle Nat was saying.

'What else was I to do?' the baron replied. 'I don't use code words lightly. This may be serious.'

'Then why involve Hal?'

'Because your nephew's powers of deduction are extraordinary. The German papers picked up the story about him solving that murder on the Safari Star.'

'He's a child, and in my care.' Uncle Nat looked troubled. 'My family don't know about my past.'

'I will not allow a hair on his head to be harmed. I swear.' The baron leaned forward. 'Nathaniel, tell me what I should do, and I will do it.' He sounded frightened. 'You two are

the best hope I have of preventing a terrible situation from escalating into a crisis.'

Uncle Nat turned his head and Hal shuffled backwards, colliding with the legs of a waiter carrying an armful of empty plates. The waiter wobbled, then, like a dancer, pivoted, regaining his balance and lifting his plates to stop them from tumbling. A single fork fell to the floor.

'*Pardon*,' Hal said, with his best French accent, jumping to his feet and returning the fork. His head was buzzing as he stumbled to the bathroom. What was in Uncle Nat's past that he didn't know about? What code word was the baron talking about? *And* what did he mean about a crisis?

CHAPTER FIVE

ENIGMA
VARIATIONS

There were two train tickets on the table when Hal returned.

'The Paris-to-Moscow express leaves Gare de l'Est this evening at 18.58 and arrives in Berlin a little after seven tomorrow morning,' the baron was saying. 'I'm afraid all the first-class compartments were booked. You'll be sharing a bedroom.'

'As long as Hal and I are together.' Uncle Nat picked up the tickets.

'Are we going to Germany, then?' Hal tried to sound casual, and did his best not to smile.

'It's up to you, Hal. If you don't want to go, we won't,' Uncle Nat said seriously.

The baron looked at Hal.

'I've drawn the family tree.' Hal held up his pocketbook. 'I'm not going home until I've solved this mystery.'

The baron looked relieved. 'I'll cover all of your expenses.'

'Well then –' Uncle Nat stood to let Hal sit back down – 'you'd better tell us who we will be masquerading as at Alexander Kratzenstein's funeral.'

'Alma has a brother, Ferdinand. He married a woman called Jessica McLain – she's Scottish, from the island of Muck in the Inner Hebrides.'

'There is never an island called Muck!' Hal exclaimed, adding Alma's brother and wife to the family tree.

'There is. I have been there,' replied the baron. 'It is mainly shoreline, seals and birds, with a tiny population of humans, barely enough people to hold a football match. Ferdinand and Jessica have a smallholding. They grow their own food and live off grid.'

'You want me to pretend to be Alma's brother?' asked Uncle Nat.

'No, he's too old. I thought you could be his daughter. She's about your age.'

Uncle Nat blinked with surprise and Hal giggled.

'Ferdinand has three children, all girls, grown up now. The middle daughter, her name is Natalie, but she is known as Nat, like you. I suggest you be Nat Strom, and Harrison be your son.'

Hal liked the idea of being disguised as Uncle Nat's son. He drew three daughters below Ferdinand and Jessica on the family tree.

'Won't anyone know that I should be female?'

'The Kratzensteins pay very little attention to the Stroms. They only like Alma because she married an influential baron.' His eyes twinkled with humour. 'A farmer on a tiny Scottish island doesn't interest them. I'd be surprised if anyone knew Ferdinand had children. When I was at Schloss Kratzenstein, I mentioned that I'd sent funeral invitations to the Stroms and that Nat Strom was coming with his son to represent that side of the family. Nobody passed comment.'

'Does it matter that I can't speak German?' Hal asked.

'No. As Harrison Strom, your grandfather would be German, and might have taught you a few words, but you would not be expected to know the language. And Nathaniel is fluent—'

'Hardly.' Uncle Nat cut him off. 'We'll need a crash course in the Strom family history before we arrive . . .'

'I have prepared a dossier for you.' He took a black plastic sleeve from the briefcase beside his chair. 'Everything you'll need is in there. And, seeing as you are going to be visiting the Brocken, may I recommend you read Goethe's *Faust*, Part One?'

'What's that?' Hal asked.

'An old play, partly set on the mountain. I think your uncle might enjoy a bit of classic German literature, although you will find it dull.' He glanced furtively at Uncle Nat. 'And Hal, you won't be the only child at the funeral. My grandchildren Hilda and Ozan will be there, as well as Alexander's sons.

'Oliver's children?' asked Uncle Nat. 'But we've met. He'll know who I am.'

'I've explained the situation to Oliver. He's more interested in the Kratzenstein library than his cousin's funeral.' He looked at Hal. 'Oliver is a scholar. Books are his first love.'

'Who else will know we're not who we're claiming to be?'

'Only Alma, Oliver and me.'

Uncle Nat frowned, and Hal was surprised by how concerned he looked.

'Nathaniel, Harrison, let me say once again how grateful I am that you two have come to my aid,' the baron said, finishing off his coffee and getting to his feet. 'I know you will uncover the truth of what is happening at Schloss Kratzenstein.' He shook Uncle Nat's hand and then Hal's. 'I will meet you in Berlin, when we will pretend not to have seen one another for many years.' He winked, and it was only after he'd left that Hal realized he'd discreetly taken care of the bill without it being brought to the table.

Uncle Nat pulled out the pages inside the black dossier. 'An old newspaper cutting about Ferdinand Strom's marriage to Jessica McClain, some typed notes about the family, which I'm guessing the baron has written for us, a map of Muck.' He rifled through the pages. 'Look, here's an old photograph of Ferdinand with his three daughters. I wonder which one I'm supposed to be?'

Hal studied the picture and then turned it over. 'There's something on the back.' He peeled off a yellow sticky note that read:

Johann Wolfgang von Goethe, Faust, Part I, trans. Elmo Grand (Macmillan, 2021), 142/3956

'That's the book the baron recommended. We'll buy a copy before we go to Gare de l'Est.'

'Won't the books here be in French?'

'I happen to know of a wonderful bookshop by Notre Dame Cathedral, set up by an American over a hundred years ago, and they sell books in English,' Uncle Nat said, sliding the pages back into the dossier. 'I'll just nip to the bathroom and then we'll get going.'

While he waited for Uncle Nat to return, Hal tucked the photograph of the Stroms into his pocketbook and flicked to the drawing he'd done of the baron and his uncle whispering over the table. What had the baron been talking about when he'd said he'd used a code word? What had he missed in that letter? His eyes flickered to his uncle's coat, which was hanging from the hatstand at the end of the banquette. The Baron's letter was in the inside pocket. It was addressed to him as well as Uncle Nat. Quick as a flash, he reached in and grabbed it. Glancing towards the bathroom, his heart lurched as Uncle Nat came out. Getting up, he quickly pulled on his yellow anorak and shoved the envelope into his pocket.

Descending into the Métro, they travelled swiftly across the city, emerging by the river Seine. Hal did up his coat to protect him against the wind, all the time uncomfortably aware of the letter in his pocket.

'Notre Dame,' Uncle Nat proclaimed, pointing at a Gothic cathedral wrapped in scaffolding. Hal recognized it from the animated *Hunchback of Notre Dame* that he had watched when he was younger.

'After we've got the book, we'll go to a *boulangerie* and get food for the journey. What do you say to a picnic dinner on the night train? We can grab a baguette, some nice cheese and a bit of fruit.'

Hal nodded. 'Brilliant.'

Shakespeare and Company was a double-fronted bookshop with a green sign, and a trolley of books outside for browsing. On a bench, in front of the shop window, sat an artist with a canvas on an easel. She was painting the cathedral. Propped up at her feet were other paintings marked with prices. It had never occurred to Hal to sell his pictures. He liked to keep the things he drew, unless he was making a gift. He wondered if it made her sad to sell them.

The bell above the door tinkled as they entered and Hal found himself inside a wonderfully higgledy-piggledy place, lined with books that spilled into nooks and round corners.

'What's *Faust* about?' Hal asked.

'A man who wants to understand the meaning of life. Unsatisfied with learning from books, Faust turns to magic and makes a deal with the devil, giving up his soul in return for one moment of experience that is so satisfactory and fulfilling that he understands what it is to be alive.'

'It's about magic?'

'Not really, although there are witches in it, and some of it takes place on the Brocken mountain, which is why the baron recommended it.'

'Is it OK if I go outside and look at the artist's painting, while you get the book?' Hal felt like the envelope was burning a hole in his pocket. He was desperate to read it.

'Of course,' Uncle Nat replied. 'I won't be long.'

Hurrying out into the street, Hal went to stand on the other side of the artist so that he was hidden from the doorway. He pulled out the baron's letter, reading it again, but couldn't see anything that looked like a code. He turned it upside down, held it up to the light, tried folding it, but saw nothing. He sighed, looking over at the artist working away at her canvas,

and a thought occurred to him: to look at the letter as if it were a drawing. He concentrated on the space in front of the letter, letting his eyes shift focus so the words became blurred, and he tried to see it as a picture. The first capital letter of each paragraph stood out and he suddenly saw that they spelled a word!

The tinkling of the shop bell shook him from his trance. He rammed the letter into his pocket, turned towards the artist's picture and arranged his face into an interested stare. But he needn't have panicked. Uncle Nat shuffled out of the door with his nose in his book.

Hal thought about the hidden word, and what he'd heard his uncle say, that his family didn't know about his past. He wondered what kind of a friendship the baron and Uncle Nat had that meant they shared a secret code.

CHAPTER SIX

THE NIGHT TRAIN TO BERLIN

When they arrived at Gare de l'Est, they were laden with food for their train picnic, and sought out two empty seats to sink into while they waited for their platform to be announced.

Hal felt uncomfortable. His uncle's secretive behaviour and the code he'd discovered in the letter made him nervous about the trip to Germany. Being left out made him feel like a child. He wanted to talk about it, but wasn't sure how. 'Uncle Nat, are you all right?'

'I'm a bit tired from travelling, but—'

'No, I mean . . .' Hal searched for the right words. 'This journey . . . it feels different from our others.'

'Yes, I suppose it is.'

'And, well . . . you're being a bit weird.' Hal struggled with words. 'You look worried all the time and you're closed off. Did I do something wrong?'

Uncle Nat's expression softened. 'Hal, you haven't done

anything wrong.' He sighed. 'You're right. This isn't like our other adventures, because I was in control of those journeys. I booked the tickets. They were supposed to be holidays. This trip is not a holiday.' He pushed his glasses up his nose. 'I'm worried about what is waiting for us in Schloss Kratzenstein. On the one hand, the baron is an important friend, and if he needs my help then I want to give it. On the other, there's the possibility that I'm taking you, one of the people I love the most, into a risky situation. I promised Bev I'd keep you safe.' He shook his head. 'Whatever I do, I feel like I'm doing the wrong thing.'

'You're not doing this alone,' Hal said firmly. 'I know I'm only twelve, but I'm here and I want to help the baron too.' He dipped his head to catch his uncle's eye. 'You can tell me *anything,* you know. I'm on your side.' Uncle Nat smiled, but didn't volunteer anything about the secret Hal knew he was keeping. 'I won't be the only child at the funeral. No one will suspect why we're there, because they'll think we're family. Neither of us thinks curses or witches are real, and if someone did kill Alexander Kratzenstein they picked a silly way to do it.'

Uncle Nat laughed. 'Unassailable logic.'

'You shouldn't worry about if you're doing the right thing – you should be preparing me for anything that might happen, by telling me *everything.*' Hal let the word hang.

Uncle Nat looked at him as if only seeing him for the first time and clapped his hand to his forehead. 'I'm being an idiot!'

'You're being a good uncle, but I need you to be the travel

writer Nathaniel Bradshaw, my friend and partner in solving crimes, because neither of us can do this alone.'

'Message understood.' Uncle Nat sat up straight and for a second Hal thought he was going to tell him the meaning of the code word: H A N G M A N, spelled out by the first letter of each paragraph in the baron's letter, but instead he pointed to the screen above their heads. 'Our train has started boarding. Let's find our compartment, eat our bread and cheese, and plot our way to Germany.'

Hal felt frustrated that Uncle Nat had changed the subject but was relieved to see the guarded look had gone from his eyes.

The Trans-European Express was a grey train with a red geometric pattern on the side. As Hal boarded the carriage, he saw that the sun was setting and marvelled that this morning he'd been in London and tomorrow he would wake up in Berlin.

Uncle Nat strode down the red-carpeted corridor to a functional compartment with four empty berths, and checked that the numbers on their tickets matched the top two bunks. He pulled out a couple of books, the brown envelope and the black dossier from his holdall, then heaved it up on to a bunk before helping Hal put his rucksack up on the other one.

They sat beside the window, opposite one another, and Uncle Nat held up a well-thumbed book entitled *Train Travel: Europe*. 'Want to see the route we're about to take?' He laid the book flat on the table between them and Hal leaned forward. 'This is us, this is northern France, and this is Germany. The train travels to Strasbourg, here, at the edge of France, where our papers will be checked. Over the border, that's Kehl. While we're sleeping, we'll travel through Frankfurt, then Erfurt, waking up in time for breakfast before arriving in Berlin.' He flipped over the page. 'It's a shame we aren't going on to Moscow. After the Polish border, they jack the train up on stilts and swap the bogies over for ones with wide wheels, because the track gauge is different there.'

'While passengers are still on board!'

'Yes,' Uncle Nat replied, enjoying Hal's surprise.

'I'd love to go to Russia one day,' Hal said wistfully as the train eased out of Gare de l'Est. Their heads turned to watch the concrete towers of the Parisian suburbs glide past the window.

'Right.' Uncle Nat slid the compartment door shut. 'Let's build our cover stories. I am Nathan Strom, Nat to my friends, and you are my only child, Harrison Strom.'

'Why Nathan?'

'If someone calls me Nathaniel, I'm liable to give myself away.'

Hal gave an involuntary shiver of excitement. 'Who is my mother? Is she dead?'

'No, the key to going undercover is creating a character and a story that are close to your own, so you can talk truthfully and with confidence about your life.' He thought for a moment. 'How about . . . your mother and I are divorced? We married too young. She's now married to a nice man called Colin and they have a baby called Ellie – your half-sister – and you all live together in Crewe. I live miles away, in Edinburgh, and you spend every other weekend with me and some of the holidays. As it's Easter, you're with me. You could even pretend to be unhappy that I've dragged you to a distant relative's funeral.'

'That's good.' Hal was impressed, and immediately felt more confident about his disguise.

'The hardest thing will be that you must always call me *Dad*. You mustn't accidentally call me *Uncle Nat* or people will become suspicious. To practise, we should start now.' Uncle Nat lifted the bag of food on to his lap and opened it. 'Are you hungry? I'm going to make sandwiches.'

'Yes please,' Hal replied, but Uncle Nat looked at him sharply. 'I mean, yes please, *Dad*.'

'Good.' Uncle Nat made his voice low and gruff. 'Show your father some respect!'

Hal giggled.

It turned out to be harder than he'd thought, remembering to call Uncle Nat *Dad* all the time. As they ate their picnic dinner, Uncle Nat went through each page of the baron's dossier, explaining how K-Bahn, the Kratzenstein family business, worked, who each member of the family was and who they could expect to meet at the funeral. Every time Hal accidentally called him Uncle Nat, he would make a bad buzzer sound and they would laugh.

They played a game called 'The Hot Seat', where they each had to answer twenty questions in character. At first, Hal made up wild, fanciful answers, but Uncle Nat pointed out that he'd blow his cover if he had to remember his favourite colour was meant to be puce when it was actually green, and suggested he stick to the truth when possible.

'The important questions to know the answers to are things like, "How do you get on with your dad?" or "How old were you when your parents split up?" . . . "Is it hard living so far away from your dad?" . . . "Do you like living with your mum?" or "Why did your dad bring you to the funeral?" . . .'

Hal got better at answering these questions and created a convincing story about how he missed his dad, because he didn't get to see him much, and he had wanted to come to the funeral to spend the holiday with his dad and visit Germany.

When it was his turn to ask Uncle Nat twenty questions, Hal was surprised by how truthful his uncle's replies sounded. 'You're a really good liar, Dad!'

'Thanks, son.' Uncle Nat looked uncomfortable. 'I prefer to think of it as acting. At university, I was a member of a drama club called Footlights. I loved it, and it taught me some useful life skills.'

It was late when the train pulled into Strasbourg. A small woman in navy trousers and poloneck, with silver-streaked black hair, entered the compartment.

'*Bonsoir*,' she said, taking a book and a green bottle from her handbag. Sitting down, she opened the bottle, took a sip and began to read.

Hal looked at Uncle Nat and pulled a face, mouthing *diabolo menthe* – the name of the drink. He had tried it in America and didn't like it. It tasted like fizzy toothpaste.

As the train left the station, a pair of border police officers came to the doorway of the compartment and asked to see their tickets and passports. Uncle Nat spoke to them in French and the woman gave him an appreciative look before showing her papers. Hal wished he could speak another language and resolved to listen in French class.

'It's getting late,' Uncle Nat said. 'We've got a big day tomorrow and an early start. Why don't you take your pyjamas and toothbrush to the bathroom, get changed and clean your teeth?'

'Yes, Dad.' Hal pulled his washbag from his rucksack.

As he headed out of the door, Uncle Nat said, 'And,

son, don't forget to wash your hands.'

Returning to the compartment, Hal was keen to clamber into his bunk. His eyes were dry, and his head heavy. He piled his stuff at his feet and pulled the blanket over himself. 'Night, Dad.'

'Night, son,' Uncle Nat replied, and they grinned at each other from their bunks.

Pulling out his copy of *Faust*, Uncle Nat propped himself up to read.

Hal wondered if he was going to struggle to drop off with the Frenchwoman sitting beneath him, but as he thought this his eyes closed.

Waking with a start, Hal's heart reeled as he failed to recognize his surroundings. He heard a terrible growl, and realized with horror that there was something in their compartment. The noise was coming from below. He peeped over the edge of his bunk. The Frenchwoman was flat on her back in the bunk below Uncle Nat, slack-jawed, mouth open. A ferocious snore ripped the air. Hal rolled back in his bed, stifling a giggle. Pulling his coat from the pile at his feet, he wrapped it round his head, but he could still hear her. He sat back up, wide awake and a little annoyed.

Uncle Nat stirred and, seeing Hal, propped himself up on his elbow. Hal covered his ears and pointed at the bunk below.

Holding up his finger, Uncle Nat reached into his duffel bag, pulled out a pouch and tossed it across the aisle to Hal. Inside was an eye mask and a pair of foam earplugs.

47

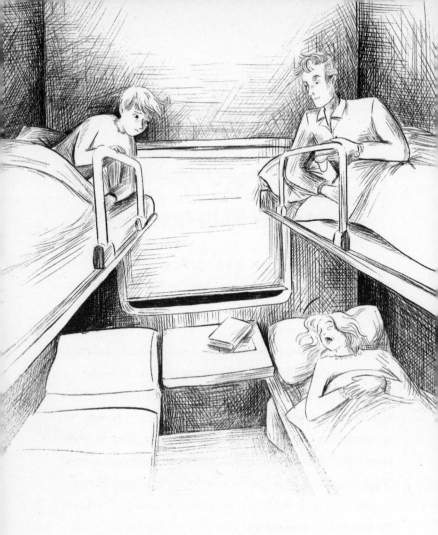

'Go back to sleep, son,' he whispered.

'Thanks, Dad,' Hal replied, sticking the earplugs in and thinking how lucky he was that his uncle knew all the tricks of travelling.

CHAPTER SEVEN

DECEPTIONS
AND DISGUISES

'Morning, son. How did you sleep?' Uncle Nat said as Hal sat up in his bunk.

The Frenchwoman was gone. Her bunk was now a seat upon which Uncle Nat was sitting, nursing a cup of coffee.

'All right, once you gave me the earplugs.' Hal threw off his blanket. 'She snored louder than my dad . . . I mean, stepdad.'

Uncle Nat laughed. 'There's a hot chocolate here for you.' He pointed at the table as Hal clambered down from his bunk. 'We'll be arriving in Berlin soon, so you'd better get dressed.'

Hal's stomach flipped as he looked out of the window. They were in Germany!

Uncle Nat seemed to know Berlin well. He led Hal from the station down to the U-Bahn, the *Untergrundbahn*, which he explained meant 'underground railway', like the Paris Métro or London Underground. They took a yellow train to Wittenbergplatz and walked for two minutes before arriving at the giant glass doors of a department store with the words *Kaufhaus Des Westens* above them.

'This is KaDeWe, the German equivalent of Harrods.'

'Are we going shopping?'

'Absolutely. Neither you nor I came with the correct clothes for a funeral, but the baron said something that has been bothering me. He mentioned that the German newspapers ran a story about you solving the case on the Safari Star. It would be a disaster if anyone recognized you as Harrison Beck. We must take precautions, so they don't.'

'How?'

'Disguise,' Uncle Nat replied, pushing the door open and ushering Hal inside. They took an escalator up to a floor exhibiting children's clothes as if they were art. Uncle Nat walked through the rails and shelves, picking up two shirts, a thick-knit cream fisherman's jumper, and a black turtleneck. He held a pair of black chinos up against Hal's body to check the size, before picking up a second pair in navy, then piled all the clothes into Hal's arms and pushed him in the direction of the fitting room.

Hal put on an outfit and looked at himself in the mirror. The clothes looked plain but felt luxurious. They weren't like the ones from the high street in Crewe. He looked at the price tag, but it was in German and he couldn't remember how much a euro was in pounds, but he guessed the clothes were expensive.

He opened the curtain, and Uncle Nat nodded his approval. 'The black jumper and trousers are for the funeral. I'll find you a jacket to go with them. The other clothes are for general wear. Keep the white shirt and fisherman's jumper on, with the blue chinos, and I'll explain at the till that you want to wear them.'

Uncle Nat selected a black suit and several polo-necks for himself, and black leather hiking boots for them both, adding thick socks to the pile. Then he picked out a wheely suitcase. 'For you,' he said to Hal. 'Put your rucksack inside it. It's scruffy.'

'Isn't this all going to cost a lot of money?'

'Yes, which is why it's a good job the baron is covering our expenses.' Uncle Nat waggled his eyebrows and Hal grinned.

On their way out, they passed through a hall of art materials. 'Wow!' Hal whispered as his eyes greedily scanned the sketchbooks and rainbow displays of pens, pencils and paints.

'I'm sorry, Hal, you can't bring anything that might give away who you really are.'

'I know.' Hal sighed. 'I'm just looking.'

'Come on, we've got to get to the barber.'

'You're getting a haircut?'

'No. You are. And I know just the man to do it. We'll grab some lunch on the way.'

They got back on the U-Bahn, this time travelling east. The line rose above the ground on stilts, offering a view of apartments and office blocks. They crossed the river Spree, getting off at the end of the line and walking to a neighbourhood called Friedrichshain, where Uncle Nat bought them currywurst – a delicious hot dog with spicy ketchup – from a street stall.

'This part of the city looks different,' Hal said as they ate and walked.

'This is East Berlin. After the Second World War, control of Germany was divided between the victors. The Soviet Union, which we now call Russia, occupied East Germany. The western democracies of Britain, France and the United States occupied West Germany. They divided Berlin, because it's the capital city, and built a wall between the two areas that you couldn't cross.'

'That doesn't sound very friendly.'

'It wasn't. For years there was tension between the East and the West and the threat of another conflict. It's known as the Cold War. It ended with the collapse of the Soviet Union in 1991. Germany was reunified and the wall was torn down.'

'And the barber is in East Berlin?'

'He is right round this corner.'

They turned into a quiet street decorated with colourful graffiti, and entered a small barbershop with a polished concrete floor, black walls and factory lighting. Uncle Nat warmly greeted a beefy, tattooed man with close-cropped blond hair and a nose ring. The two men hugged, and Hal was startled to hear Uncle Nat talking in fluent German. He pointed to Hal, and the barber studied him, speaking while counting on his fingers.

'What's he saying?' Hal was suddenly nervous.

'Karl says we can either dye your hair dark and crop it short, or make a centre parting and shave the sides . . .'

Hal looked at Uncle Nat in horror. 'I'll look like an idiot!'

'Or we trim the sides and curl your fringe and the longer hair on top.'

'Curl it?'

'Your hair would stay its natural colour, but you'd have a curly fringe.' He nodded. 'You'd look completely different.'

'Do you mean a *perm*?' Hal imagined the look on Ben's face if he went home with curly hair. 'What about when I go back to school?'

'It'd be a semi-permanent curl. After a few washes, it falls out.'

'My hair?'

Uncle Nat laughed. 'No, the curls drop out. Your hair goes back to being straight.'

'OK, let's do that.' Hal sat in the leather chair and stared into the mirror as Karl wheeled over a black trolley loaded with rollers, silver foil segments and bottles of chemicals. He watched with fear and fascination as the man sectioned his hair, covered it in pungent liquid from a squirty bottle and wound it round a roller that he secured with a piece of foil and a clip.

'I've got to run an errand,' Uncle Nat said. 'I'll be back in twenty minutes.'

When he returned, Hal's head was inside a heated helmet. Uncle Nat stood behind him to watch Karl remove the rollers. Hal couldn't help but giggle at the sight of his hair in corkscrew noodles. His head was washed, conditioned, the sides were cut, the edges shaved into a neat line, and then Karl blow-dried and scrunched Hal's hair until a bunch of curls dangled

53

over his forehead, sweeping down over his right eye.

'These are for you.' Uncle Nat handed Hal a little white bag with a black oblong case inside. Hal opened it to find a pair of thick-framed tortoiseshell glasses, like Uncle Nat's, but smaller.

'They have clear lenses,' Uncle Nat said. 'Try them on.'

Hal stared at the reflection of an intelligent-looking, well-groomed and wealthy boy in the mirror. 'I don't believe it,' he whispered, leaning in to study his face. The shorter hair at the sides made his face look longer and more angular. The glasses defended his eyes from the dangling curls and hid the shape of his nose. 'Mum wouldn't even recognize me like this.'

'Yes she would. There's no disguise you could put on that would fool your mother.'

As his uncle followed Karl to the till, Hal took out his pocketbook and drew a quick self-portrait.

'My name's Harrison Strom,' he said to the mirror. 'Pleased to meet you.'

Karl let them use a room at the back of the shop to sort out their belongings and cut the price tags from Hal's clothes. By the time they walked out on to the street, Hal felt like a new person. Uncle Nat hailed a taxi and gave the address for Alexander Kratzenstein's apartment.

'There's no turning back once we've met the Kratzensteins,' Uncle Nat said as they got in.

'I'm ready, Dad,' Hal replied, trying to ignore the booming heartbeat in his ears. He caught his reflection in the taxi window and for a second didn't recognize himself, which stabilized his wobbling confidence. Realizing he was still wearing his silver train whistle, he took it off and slipped it into his trouser pocket.

'This is it,' Uncle Nat said as the taxi pulled up in front of a grand, white, stone-fronted building. 'Are you ready, Harrison?'

'Yes, Dad, I'm ready.'

CHAPTER EIGHT

FAMILY GATHERING

Uncle Nat pressed the buzzer and after a pause the door clicked and opened, revealing a cavernous lobby with a marble floor and a grand staircase climbing round a lift shaft of wrought iron. Hal pushed his glasses up his nose as they stepped inside. A high whirring indicated the lift was descending. The lattice gate was pulled open by a smartly dressed woman in a dark dress with pinned-back hair.

'*Guten Tag*,' she said. 'Herr Strom?'

'*Ja*,' Uncle Nat replied.

'*Wilkommen*.' The woman ushered them in and pulled the gate shut.

They rose up to the fourth floor, stopping in front of a wooden door as large as the entrance to the building. The woman went ahead of them and Hal heard music as she opened the door, a high melancholy tune. Uncle Nat's hand on his back steered him down an ocean-blue hallway. Glancing through an open door, Hal saw a pale, silver-haired boy, dressed in black, sitting at a grand piano. He was young to be playing such a complicated piece. *That must be Herman,* Hal thought, *Alexander Kratzenstein's youngest son.*

At the sound of their footsteps Herman stopped playing and turned. His eyes were ringed with purple shadows. Hal raised his hand in greeting, but the boy dropped his head and carried on playing.

The next room was the size of Hal's school hall. Tall panelled windows threw sunlight on to exposed brick walls, and a giant dining table set for dinner. A balcony overlooked the street. On the wall hung three huge canvases covered in thick white paint. Dark smudged shapes in the middle were splattered with red and orange. A woman with almond-shaped blue eyes, and a smattering of freckles across her elven face, got up from a low settee. She swept her long fair hair back over her shoulders as she rose, and her black chiffon dress billowed delicately.

Herman Kratzenstein

Hal knew immediately that this was Herman's mum, Clara – Alexander's second wife. She was beautiful.

'*Guten Tag, Frau Kratzenstein*,' Uncle Nat said, stepping forward.

'Oh no, let us speak English.' She clasped his outstretched hand with both of hers. 'It's good to meet you.' She turned to Hal. 'And you must be Harrison. Wolfgang tells me you don't speak German, so it would be rude for us to.'

'Thank you,' Hal replied, remembering that Wolfgang was the baron's name.

'Do you play an instrument, Harrison?' Clara asked hopefully. 'Herman's learning Bach.'

'I play the recorder, but not very well.'

'It was kind of you to invite us to dinner today,' Uncle Nat said. 'This is the first time Harrison is meeting his German family. I only wish it could have been under happier circumstances. I am very sorry for your loss, Frau Kratzenstein.'

'Oh!' A sharp line of distress appeared in the centre of Clara's forehead and her lip trembled. 'Thank you, but you must call me Clara.' She pushed her lips together as her eyes filled with tears. 'And, please, don't be too kind or I shall cry, and my face will go all red and puffy.'

'Kind? Me?' Uncle Nat pretended to frown. 'Impossible. I'm a perfect monster. Just ask Harrison's mother.'

Clara laughed gratefully. 'Let me show you to your rooms.' She took Uncle Nat's arm and walked beside him. 'Harrison, I've put you in with your cousins, Ozan and Hilda.' She looked up at Nat. 'You are in our smallest guest room. I'm afraid the apartment is full.'

'Are Wolfgang and Alma here?'

'They went out, but will be back for dinner. Do you know Oliver? He's upstairs. And Arnie's here too.'

'Arnie came from Wernigerode?' Uncle Nat said casually, giving the impression he knew him.

Clara leaned close. 'I think his mother has sent him to make sure I don't sell the silver before the will is read. She is controlling Alexander's father using that nurse she hired to take care of him, but she can't control me.'

Hal felt a jolt at the mention of the will. Did Clara not know it was missing?

'Arnie brought the family train to Berlin for us to travel back in,' added Clara.

'You have your own train?' Hal asked.

'Yes. It's an old-fashioned thing, but Alexander loved it. He was the last person to use it, when he went to Wernigerode...' She paused and Hal could tell she was trying not to cry.

'You have a lovely home,' Uncle Nat said, tactfully changing the subject.

'Thank you.' Clara smiled. 'The changing sky is my palette for the walls. Each room is a different shade of blue, and the earth inspires my floors.' She rested a hand delicately on the iron balustrade as she climbed the stairs. 'We own three floors of this building, but only live on this one and the one above. The top-floor apartment I offer to artists who wish to come and make work inspired by Berlin's rich culture.'

'Very generous of you,' Uncle Nat said.

'Harrison, this is where you'll be sleeping.' Clara opened

the door to a teal room with a thick sandy carpet. Sitting on a pair of twin beds were a boy with a mop of unruly locks and a girl with long straight dark hair. They stared inquisitively at Hal.

'Hi,' Hal said awkwardly.

'Lina will make up a bed for you and bring up your case,' Clara said, closing the door.

'Are you our cousin from Scotland?' asked the boy.

'No. I mean, yes, but I don't live in Scotland. Not most of the time.' Hal felt himself getting hot. 'I don't think we're actually cousins. We're twice removed or something.'

'Cousins is easier,' the boy pointed out. His accent was strong, but his English was surprisingly good.

'Yes.' The girl smiled. 'Let's be cousins.'

'OK.'

'I'm Ozan.' The boy shook Hal's hand. 'And you are Harrison. Opa told us about you.'

'I'm Hilda.' She scrambled off the bed, clutching a yellow book called *Emil and the Detectives*, her finger marking her page.

'Isn't this funeral great?' Ozan said,

Hilda Essenbach

enthusiastically. 'We get to go to Schloss Kratzenstein and meet our cousins.'

'Um . . .' Hal wasn't sure how to respond.

'And the adults will be far too busy to tell us what to do,' Ozan added.

'Papa says Schloss Kratzenstein is haunted,' Hilda said with glee. 'And the library is so big it has ladders on rails.'

'*Pfff!*' Ozan rolled his eyes. 'Harrison doesn't want to look at books when Großonkel Arnold has a model railway to rival Opa's.'

'Opa has the best model railway in the world,' Hilda replied sniffily, taking offence on his behalf.

Hal guessed that Opa meant Grandpa, as he knew the baron's model railway was famous.

There was a knock, and Lina wheeled Hal's case in. The children got out of her way as she expertly took out a mattress from beneath one of the beds, pulled it up to the same height, and clothed it with white linen.

'*Danke schön,*' Hal said, hoping it sounded right, and Lina smiled as she left. To his embarrassment, his stomach growled loudly, and he put his hand over his belly.

'Are you hungry?' a voice whispered at his ear.

'*Gahhh!*' Hal nearly jumped out of his skin. He spun round to find Herman standing right behind him. 'You frightened me!' he snapped, and Herman slunk backwards towards the door.

'Don't go.' Hilda ran to him and took his hand, pulling him

to Ozan's bed and sitting him down. 'I'm Hilda, your cousin.'

Herman rewarded her with a timid smile. 'I came to say hello.' His voice was rasping, and his chest wheezed as he breathed in.

'I'm sorry I shouted at you,' Hal said. 'I didn't hear you come in.'

'Herman is stealthy, like a cat,' Ozan said, sounding impressed.

'If you're hungry,' Herman said, 'I will ask Lina to send up snacks to the playroom?'

'I am a bit hungry,' Hal admitted.

'Me too,' agreed Hilda.

'Go to the room at the end of the hall,' Herman said, hurrying to the door. 'I'll be back in a minute.'

The playroom was the only room in the apartment that wasn't blue. It was white, and it looked lived in. Although toys and games were stacked neatly on shelves, there was Lego scattered on the floor in front of the TV.

Hal and Hilda dropped on to the two sofas, but Ozan sat down on the floor beside the Lego and began pressing the bricks together.

Herman came in carrying a bowl of crisps. 'What are you making?'

'*Die Rakotzbrücke*,' Ozan replied, and then for Hal's benefit added, 'It's a famous bridge.'

'That's specific.' Hal was intrigued. Without instructions, he only ever made brightly coloured square houses or space vehicles.

'Ozan is always specific,' Hilda said, rolling her eyes.

'You will be glad that I am when I invent a robot that saves lives one day, or design a bridge –' he held up the Lego – 'that crosses into another dimension and—'

Hilda turned away from her brother, cutting him off. 'Herman, I heard you playing the piano when we arrived. You are very good.'

'I was practising.' Herman's pale cheeks

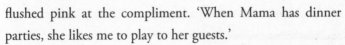

Ozan Essenbach

flushed pink at the compliment. 'When Mama has dinner parties, she likes me to play to her guests.'

'Is she going to make you play to us?' Hal asked, horrified on his behalf.

'Do you want us to get you out of it?' Ozan offered.

'It's OK.' Herman smiled at their concern. 'It makes Mama happy.'

'Does everyone speak English in Germany?' asked Hal, amazed that Herman could do it so well at the age of nine.

'Does no one speak German in England?' Ozan replied, laughing.

'We're not taught it at my school,' Hal admitted.

63

'Ozan and I go to an international school. Mama is Turkish and Papa is German, so we speak both languages at home. At school they use English, but I also speak French and Spanish.'

'You're multilingual?' Hal felt inadequate.

'I don't speak French and Spanish very well,' Ozan said, 'but I make up for it with the universal languages of maths and science.'

Hilda groaned.

'I'm tutored at home,' Herman said. 'I've always been taught English.'

'Learning languages is like decoding secret messages,' said Hilda. 'It's fun. When I grow up, I'm going to be a translator like Mama.'

'When I get home, I'm going to ask for German lessons,' Hal said.

'What kinds of things do you like?' Ozan asked.

'I'm into . . .' Hal wanted to tell them he loved drawing and travelling. 'Sport.'

'What do you play?' Ozan asked, immediately interested.

'Football. I play for the school team,' Hal said, remembering what Uncle Nat said about sticking to the truth. 'I'm a midfielder.'

'I can't do much sport because of my asthma,' said Herman.

Lina entered with a tray of four mini burgers in buns and a plate of pickles, and they all cheered. She handed it to Herman, winked and left.

'*Hey, Kotzbrocken, was machst du?*' A lanky young man, not capable of growing more than a fuzz of facial hair, was lounging against the door frame.

'What did he say?' Hal asked Ozan quietly.

'He said, *What are you doing, you lump of puke?*' Ozan replied under his breath.

'Ar-Arnie,' Herman stuttered.

Arnie sloped into the room and grabbed two mini burgers from Herman's plate, stuffing them into his mouth at the same time, and chewed with his mouth open, surveying the four children as if they were stray dogs.

Sitting forward and smiling sweetly, Hilda said, 'Hello, Arnie, I'm Hilda. We've decided to speak English because Harrison doesn't know German.'

'*Herzlich willkommen, Engländer*,' Arnie snorted, but he switched to English. 'Don't eat too many of these.' He picked up the other two burgers on the plate.

'Dinner is six courses, and we don't want to upset Clara, do we?' He stuffed the burgers into his mouth, opened it wide so they could all see the chewed-up food, then walked out.

Hal looked at Herman. 'That's your brother?'

'Half-brother,' Herman wheezed through gritted teeth.

Arnie Kratzenstein

CHAPTER NINE

A DREADFUL DINNER

A gong summoned them to dinner and the hungry children scurried down the stairs, bumping into Hilda and Ozan's dad.

'Papa, meet Harrison,' Hilda said, grabbing Hal's arm.

'Pleased to meet you.' Oliver smiled warmly at Hal, winking almost imperceptibly as he shook his hand, to show he understood who he really was. Oliver Essenbach was fairer than his brother Milo, whom Hal had met on the Highland Falcon. He had a neat beard, glasses, and there was a twinkle in his hazel eyes, which made Hal instinctively like him.

He herded the children to the dinner table, where Uncle Nat, the baron, and his wife Alma were already seated.

'Harrison, come and give your great-aunty a big hug,' Alma said, getting to her feet. 'I haven't seen you since you were a baby.' She enveloped him in a cuddle of white cashmere cardigan and lavender perfume, whispering, 'Thank you for coming,' in his ear. When she smiled, Alma Essenbach had a habit of lifting her shoulders, which, despite her greying curly mane, made her seem girlish.

Hal was pleased to find he'd been seated between Uncle Nat and Ozan.

'How're you settling in?' Uncle Nat asked him as he sat down.

'Good,' Hal replied, as Lina entered with the first course.

Throughout the meal, Arnie was insufferable. He would take one mouthful of a dish and proclaim it over-seasoned, or tasteless, saying he was unable to eat it. Hal, Herman, Ozan and Hilda knew his stomach was full with their mini burgers. Clara ignored Arnie's rudeness, which made him behave more outrageously. Eventually the baron intervened, commenting that a gentleman should know how to enjoy fine cuisine and compliment their host, whilst shooting a withering look at Arnie who sat up straight and ate the rest of his food in a sulky silence.

Clara asked Uncle Nat about life on the island of Muck, and he explained apologetically that growing up tending to pigs, goats and chickens had made him long for an urban life, and as soon as he'd got old enough, he'd moved to Edinburgh.

'My brother has the soul of a farmer,' Alma said, 'but it's hard work and not for everyone.'

'Precisely,' Uncle Nat agreed, then deftly changed the subject. 'Wolfgang, I hope you don't mind my asking, but what are the arrangements for travelling to the funeral? Can I be of any assistance?'

'We take the family train tomorrow to Schloss Kratzenstein. The funeral home is taking care of Alexander. People will be able to pay their last respects in person, at the house, on Sunday. The funeral is of course on Monday.' The baron put his hand over Clara's and smiled sadly.

'I wish I could bring him home to Berlin,' she said in a whisper.

'He *is* at home,' Arnie said moodily. '*His* family home.'

'There is a long-held family tradition,' the baron said, ignoring Arnie, 'that the Kratzensteins are buried in their mausoleum on the estate.

The German government has rigid rules about funerals, but, as a person of influence, I was able to secure the permissions needed to proceed with the funeral in the traditional way, in accordance with the family's wishes.'

Clara frowned, looking puzzled.

'The mausoleum is near the peak of the Brocken.' Alma shuddered. 'The funeral train gave me nightmares when I was a girl.'

'Funeral train?' Hal prompted, hoping she'd say more.

'It carries the family's dead to the mausoleum. The Kratzensteins don't use a hearse or a black carriage – they use the funeral train.' She lowered her voice. 'In defiance of the curse.'

'What curse?' Hilda whispered, leaning forward.

'Don't you know?' Arnie sneered. 'Kratzenstein men are cursed to die unnatural deaths, before their time.' He sat back. 'I could die tomorrow.' He looked sombrely at Herman. 'And so could you.'

Clara clapped her hands over Herman's ears. 'That's not true.'

'Isn't it?' Arnie stuck his chin forward, wearing an expression of defiance. 'What about Uncle Manfred? He was only a few years older than me when he died. And how do you explain what happened to my father?' He shook his head. 'Strange things are taking place at the Kratzenstein house.'

'What strange things?' Hal asked, and he wasn't the only person who leaned forward to hear the answer.

'The house is haunted,' Arnie replied. 'I'm not the only one who thinks it. Opa does too. The witch is coming for him.'

'I'm sure that's not true,' Uncle Nat said, trying to be reassuring.

'There was a night of storms in January, and we were woken by a crashing noise. In the morning, Opa's portrait – the one

70

that hangs in the long gallery with the other family pictures – was face down on the floor, the frame smashed.'

'A picture hook probably gave way,' Oliver suggested, but Arnie shook his head.

'We've seen her.'

'Seen who?' Hal asked.

'The witch who cursed the Kratzensteins.'

'Who has seen her?' Uncle Nat asked.

'All of us. Mama, Me, Opa and Connie.'

'Who's Connie?' Hal asked.

'Opa's nurse. She went for a hike in the mountains, but on her way home through the woods an icy fog descended and she lost her path and came into a clearing. She saw the guts of a rodent on a rock, and beyond them the hooded figure of a woman holding up a bloody knife.'

Hal put his fork down, suddenly losing his appetite.

'There are no such things as witches,' said the baron.

'There are in Wernigerode,' Alma replied quietly.

'What happened next?' Hal asked.

'That is the strangest thing. The witch took a step back and vanished.' Arnie flicked his fingers out. 'Connie said she became mist.'

'People don't just vanish,' Ozan said nervously, looking at his dad.

'A trick of the weather,' the baron said, 'and an overactive imagination.'

'She was casting a spell,' Arnie insisted, 'to bring Dad to Dead Man's Pass, so that she could kill him.'

A high wailing sound came from Herman, who had his eyes screwed tightly shut and his hands over his ears.

'Arnold!' Clara snapped. 'That's enough.' She moved her chair closer to Herman and put her arms round him.

'Yes, let's change the subject,' Uncle Nat agreed. 'I'm sure the nurse was mistaken in what she saw. There will be a logical explanation.'

'But I've seen the witch too,' Arnie said defiantly. 'Twice!'

'Did she try and get you?' Ozan asked.

'The first time I saw her, I was helping Aksel clear the tracks in Dead Man's Pass. Sometimes the snow causes rockfalls. I was bent over, throwing stones clear of the tracks, when I got a crick in my neck. I looked up and saw a woman in a grey hood above us on the mountain. She was watching us. I blinked and she was gone.'

'The witch!' Ozan said.

'It could have been anyone,' Hilda said, unimpressed.

'A few weeks later, I was returning home from visiting friends. It was late and dark. I didn't want to go through the woods, so I followed the railway line through Dead Man's Pass. I was walking fast, but over the sound of my breath and my footsteps I heard a strange chanting. I stopped to listen. It was a woman's voice, speaking a language I did not know. She sounded as if her mouth was full of marbles. I crept closer to the sound and saw the skull face in the pass glowing with a ghostly light.' Herman gasped at this. 'I couldn't see anyone, but I moved closer to where the strange chanting was coming from . . .' His voice became a whisper and they leaned

72

towards him. 'And then I felt a terrible chill in my heart, like it had been stabbed with ice, and the chanting fell silent.' His eyes were wide. 'I sensed someone behind me. I spun round and . . . *Rrrroooaaarrrrr!*' Arnie lurched forward, howling.

Hal jumped.

Herman screamed and Clara gasped.

Hilda jumped to her feet and Ozan cried out, moving backwards so fast he fell off his chair.

Arnie's howls dissolved into peals of laughter.

'Arnold, that was very childish,' the baron scolded gently.

'You should have seen your faces.' Arnie pointed, unable to stop laughing. 'You were terrified!'

'Did you decide to frighten everyone,' Uncle Nat said quietly, 'to distract from the fact that you did see a woman that night, got scared and ran away?'

Arnie's laughter died in his throat and Hal could see this was true.

Uncle Nat glanced at the baron, and Hal noticed they exchanged a look.

The rest of the dinner passed in a tense exchange of talk about nothing in particular. Hal's fingers ached to draw. He wanted to sketch the arrogant angle of Arnie's head, the worried lines around Alma's kind eyes, the drawn features of beautiful Clara and the haunted Herman. He was desperate to talk to his uncle about the witch, but after dessert the children were instructed to go upstairs and get ready to bed.

As they got up to leave, Arnie stuck his tongue out at them.

'Shouldn't Arnie come with us?' Ozan asked loudly. 'He behaves like a child.'

'Want to play a board game in the playroom?' Hilda whispered as they climbed the stairs.

'Can we play Catan?' Herman looked delighted.

'I'm tired.' Hal faked a yawn. 'I didn't sleep well on the train last night. I'm going to go to bed.' He wished them goodnight, but instead of going to the bedroom he went to the bathroom at the top of the stairs and locked the door.

Sitting on the toilet, he pulled out his pocketbook and drew the dinner party, all the while listening for the sound of adults going to bed. When he heard noises downstairs, he watched through a gap in the door, hoping to see Uncle Nat pass, but there was no sign of him, so he decided to go downstairs and look for him.

The dining room was dark and empty. Hearing a distant click, Hal went to the window, then opened the door on to the balcony, gasping as an icy wind slapped his face. Below him in the street, he saw a furtive figure silhouetted by a streetlight. Uncle Nat was walking fast, keeping to the shadows. Hal pulled out his pocketbook and drew his uncle hurrying away into the night.

CHAPTER TEN

ZUG KRATZENSTEIN

Hal overslept, waking to find the apartment in a flurry of activity. Everyone was getting dressed and packed. Oliver Essenbach appeared at the bedroom door just as Ozan flung his pillow at Hilda.

'Ozan, now is not the time to pick a fight with your sister. The bus has arrived to take us to the station. Hurry yourselves up and make sure you don't leave anything.'

Hal sprang up and threw on his clothes. He stuffed his pyjamas into his suitcase and zipped it up.

'Are you coming?' Hilda said, dragging her bag past the foot of his bed.

'I've got to speak to my un—' Hal caught himself. 'My dad. Be down in a second.'

'Don't forget your glasses.' Ozan pointed to the bedside table.

'I won't,' Hal replied, picking them up and putting them on, inwardly scolding himself for forgetting he was in disguise. He'd better not do that again.

Hurrying to Uncle Nat's room, he found the door open. His uncle was standing with his back to the door, putting a pile of neatly folded shirts into his holdall. His copy of *Faust* was on the bed; the spine was cracked and a piece of paper stuck out of it, marking a page. With a lurch, Hal suddenly remembered that he still had the baron's letter in his coat pocket. He whipped it out and slipped it into the inside pocket of Uncle Nat's coat, which was hanging on the back of the door.

Clara's moonlike face poked round the corner. 'We're all downstairs. It is time to board the bus to the station.'

'We're coming,' Hal replied.

'Ah, Harrison, are you packed?' Uncle Nat zipped his bag and grabbed his coat. 'Good. Let's go.'

Hal needed to talk to his uncle. 'Dad . . . About last night.'

'We don't have time to go into it now,' Uncle Nat said in a low voice. 'Let's talk this evening, at Schloss Kratzenstein, when we have some privacy.' He met Hal's eyes and Hal nodded, though he thought he might burst from waiting.

Out on the pavement, Ozan and Hilda were bickering. Ozan had Hilda's book and was threatening to read the last chapter out loud and ruin the ending. Hilda had jammed her fingers in her ears and was singing loudly. Herman, dressed in a thick black woollen coat that reached down to his knees, was watching them.

'*Guten Morgen, Arsch mit Ohren*,' Arnie said, striding past Hal and ruffling Herman's hair.

'Maybe Arnie's decided to be nicer today,' Hal said to Ozan.

'He said, *Good morning, ass with ears*,' Ozan replied. 'It means *idiot*.'

'He's not a nice brother,' Hal observed, feeling sorry for the miserable-looking Herman.

'All brothers are horrible,' Hilda said, glaring at Ozan, who waved her book.

They climbed on to the bus, the four children claiming the back seat, and Hal found himself beside Herman. 'Are you looking forward to the train ride?' he asked cheerily.

Herman shook his head. 'The train is taking me to my death.' He looked at Hal with mournful eyes and whispered, 'I'm cursed.'

'Herman, you mustn't believe in this curse,' Hal said softly. 'Arnie is being mean and winding you up.'

'He isn't.' Herman's grey eyes were wide. 'Can't you tell? He's frightened too.'

Hal paused, realizing Herman was right. 'How about I promise to protect you?' he said, poking Ozan and looking at Hilda. 'We'll all look out for you, Herman, won't we?' They nodded. 'We are cousins, after all.'

'Yes,' Ozan and Hilda replied. 'Of course.'

Herman pushed his lips into a thin smile.

When they arrived at Berlin Hauptbahnhof station, the family trooped on to an escalator. Hal gazed up through the floors of shops and railway lines, impressed by the futuristic station with its blue glass roof arching high above him like a cresting wave of ice.

The platform was empty but for two middle-aged women

standing beside a cat basket. One was dressed in a navy trouser suit and camel-coloured coat, her black hair cropped close to her dark brown skin. The other woman was pale with pink flushed cheeks. Her wavy mane of thick dark hair was streaked with grey and pinned up either side of her head with coral combs. She wore dangly gold earrings, purple eyeshadow and at least five different-length necklaces over a gold-and-black blouse that shimmered beneath her fluffy faux-fur green coat. She looked a little magical.

As the family moved towards them, Hal noticed the eccentric-looking woman nervously take the other's hand.

Arnie glared at them. 'Those stupid women are on the wrong platform,' he said, and marched towards them, his chin jutting forward as he called out, '*Was denkt ihr, dass ihr hier macht?*'

Oliver hurried after Arnie with an apologetic look on his face.

'*Wer von euch ist Clara Kratzenstein?*' the eccentric-looking woman asked, her eyes flitting from Alma to Clara with a questioning look.

'I am Clara Kratzenstein.'

The woman let go of her friend's hand and hugged Clara to her. '*Schwester, mein herzliches Beileid,*' the woman said. '*Ich bin Freya.*'

'Freya?' Clara blinked. 'Alexander's sister?'

Freya nodded. 'I'm sorry I did not come to your wedding. If I had, this wouldn't be so strange.'

'Aunt Freya?' Arnie looked confused. 'You're coming to Wernigerode?'

'Yes, young Arnold,' Freya replied, turning and cupping his cheek with her hands. 'I haven't seen you since you were a chubby baby. You look like your father, though I see Bertha in your chin and behind those eyes.'

'People call me Arnie,' he said grudgingly.

'Well, it is nice to see you again, Arnie.' She looked around. 'Why are we speaking English?'

'That's my fault,' Uncle Nat said, extending his hand. 'Nathan Strom. Your second cousin.' They shook hands. 'My German is not very good, and my son, Harrison –' he extended his arm and Hal stepped to his side – 'speaks no more than a handful of words.'

'Cousin Freya,' Alma gushed, hugging her. 'We can't have been more than children when last we met, but you haven't changed.'

The smartly dressed woman had been hanging back, but Freya grabbed her arm and pulled her forward. 'Alma, everyone, this is Rada, my partner. She's joining us for the weekend.'

'Lovely to meet you, Rada.' Alma hugged her too.

'Oh, I'm so happy you're here,' Clara declared with tear-filled eyes, linking her arm through Freya's. 'It will be good to have a sister at Schloss Kratzenstein.'

As Hal watched the women walking down the platform, he realized that Clara was dreading the trip to the house almost as much as Herman.

'Look there! It's here!' Ozan called out as a square sky-blue locomotive, pulling three old-fashioned carriages, approached the platform. The carriages were short, panelled with dark wood and ringed with curling ironwork. One even had a chimney.

'A Bombardier TRAXX,' Uncle Nat muttered appreciatively.

'Electric,' Hal said, seeing the pantograph that reached up

from the top of the train making contact with the overhead power line.

'Diesel-electric and, I think by the model number, dual-voltage. That loco can travel anywhere.'

'As long as their wheels match the track gauge,' Hal added in a knowing tone, and Uncle Nat laughed.

'Yes, but I'll bet it has a variable gauge system, so all you'd need to do is to pass through a gauge changer.'

'The carriages look ancient.'

'Early 1900s. Wooden, with welded steel underframe. Beautiful. They're short so they can travel on winding narrow-gauge tracks through mountains.'

Hal wished he could draw the train. Two men in station uniforms began loading their luggage into the end coach, and the train driver had opened his door to talk to Arnie. He was burly, with thick dark brows and hairy arms and hands. He wore charcoal overalls unbuttoned to reveal a plaid shirt and red bandana. Arnie climbed up into the cabin, sitting down beside the driver, and Hal felt a pang of envy.

'What do you make of Freya Kratzenstein?' Hal asked his uncle quietly. 'No one's mentioned her before. She's not on my family tree.'

'She's Alexander's sister. There was some falling-out in the family when she was young. The baron must have invited her as a courtesy. I don't think anyone expected her to show up.'

'That's suspicious, don't you think?' Hal said. 'Alexander dies in strange circumstances, his will goes missing and then she suddenly turns up?'

'It's certainly interesting,' Uncle Nat agreed. 'Come on, we'd better board the train. We're the only ones left on the platform.'

Ozan and Hilda waved at Hal from a carriage door, grabbing and pulling him on to the train.

'This way,' Hilda said.

'What took you so long?' Ozan asked.

'Dad and I were admiring the train.' Hal turned and Uncle Nat waved at him and went into the next carriage. There'd been a moment on the platform when he'd thought Uncle Nat and he were finally going to talk about their investigation, but again their conversation had been cut short.

'Herman, how come Arnie gets to ride in the cab with the driver?' Hal asked, following Ozan into a carriage decorated like a grand office.

'Aksel Mulch is the groundsman at Schloss Kratzenstein,' Herman replied, sitting on a sofa. 'He takes care of Opa's trains. He's been at the house since he was a boy. His mother used to be the housekeeper.' He looked out of the window. 'But she's dead now.'

Ozan grimaced at Hal, who struggled not to laugh.

They felt the familiar jerk of the train moving out of the platform, and as it emerged from the shelter of the blue glass roof the grey light of morning flooded the carriage. Picking up speed, they rattled past the tower blocks of Berlin, finally on their way to Schloss Kratzenstein.

83

CHAPTER ELEVEN

BELLADONNA

Alexander Kratzenstein's private train told of his pride in the family railway business. On the walls of his travelling office, between windows fitted with wooden blinds, were antique posters celebrating a hundred years of German railways, 1824 to 1924, framed and bolted to the varnished wooden walls. The carriage was stripped of any usual fittings; it had no corridor, and was laid with a thick burgundy carpet. Down the far end was a heavy wooden desk with an anglepoise lamp and a cast-iron model of a Class 99 steam locomotive on it. Behind it was a high-backed leather chair and a fitted bookshelf that filled the end wall. In the centre of the shelves hung a portrait of Alexander Kratzenstein himself. He looked severe, sour and powerful. Wherever Hal was standing in the carriage, the picture seemed to be looking at him.

The children sat on two sofas facing each other. Between them was a table on which stood the heavy black and white soldiers of a marble chess set. Hal noticed that Herman had chosen to sit with his back to his father's picture. It occurred to him that Alexander Kratzenstein would have been sitting at his desk only eight days ago, on his way to Schloss Kratzenstein, and he shuddered. He leaned his forehead against the glass of the window, watching the agricultural land of Germany zip by. A rusty mound beside the track caught his eye, and he recoiled at the sight of a dead fox.

'What is it?' Herman asked.

'Nothing,' Hal replied with a forced smile. 'I'd love to look at the other carriages in the train. Do you want to show me around?'

Herman paused then shook his head.

Hal nodded, glancing at the empty chair behind the desk, trying to avoid the piercing eyes of the painting. Being on this train was upsetting Herman, and it was creeping him out too. He was beginning to dread what he might find waiting for him at Schloss Kratzenstein.

Ozan jumped up, saying, 'I'll come with you,' and Hal wondered if he too was finding this carriage unsettling.

'I'll stay with Herman,' Hilda said.

'You can go with them if you want,' Herman said mournfully.

'I don't.' She held up her book. 'I want to finish this before Ozan ruins it.'

'I can tell you the ending right now.' Ozan grinned.

'Unless you want to play chess?' Hilda said to Herman, ignoring her brother.

'Come on, Ozan.' Hal went to the carriage door and opened it. There wasn't a corridor to the next car, but instead an outdoor veranda. The boys exchanged a gleeful look, gripping the railing tightly as they crossed to the opposite platform, buffeted by the wind and exhilarated by the speed of the train.

'Whoever takes care of these carriages does a good job,' Ozan shouted. 'They're a hundred years old, but nothing rattles.'

Stumbling into the next carriage, they were embraced by warmth and the smell of coffee. The adults all stopped talking and looked at them.

The room in which they found themselves made Hal think of a log cabin. Mounted on the rust-red walls was a glassy-eyed stag's head. At the far end of the room was a cylindrical wood-burning stove with a silver chimney piping smoke out through the roof, and the floor was covered with a thick patterned rug of russet and gold.

'Hi,' he said, conscious that they'd burst in on something they weren't supposed to hear. He wondered if they'd been discussing the funeral.

There were two upholstered sofas along the far wall. Uncle Nat and Oliver Essenbach were perched on one, Alma and Clara were on the other. The baron was in a chunky wooden armchair opposite them, and Rada in one close to the stove, sipping coffee. Freya was sitting at her feet, with the black cat on her lap, stroking and fussing over it.

'Is Herman all right?' Clara asked.

'He's playing chess with Hilda,' Ozan replied. 'Harrison wanted to look around the train.'

Hal blushed.

'Harrison,' Freya said, 'in this family we're all train crazy. You must explore every inch of this train if you want to.'

'Thank you,' Hal replied gratefully, noticing that Freya was the only grown-up who didn't look tense or worried. She was smiling warmly at him and her eyes twinkled, and before he'd considered whether it was rude or not he said, 'Freya, do you believe in the witch's curse? The Kratzenstein curse, I mean?'

Everyone in the carriage stiffened and looked at her.

'What is a witch?' Freya's voice was husky. 'That is a good question. Many years ago the Kratzensteins did something terrible, and were cursed for it.' She paused, drawing in a long breath. 'Do I believe the words of a curse have the power to kill?' She slowly shook her head. 'Words cannot kill on their own.'

'Please, let's not talk about the curse,' Alma said, wringing her hands. 'My mother was a Kratzenstein.'

'Don't be frightened, Oma,' Ozan said, taking a poker from a hook on the wall and making his way to the wood burner. 'Science can prove curses can't hurt you.' He opened the door and prodded the glowing embers, then put another log in.

'It hurt my Alexander,' whispered Clara.

Everybody looked down, not knowing what to say.

Uncle Nat began a quiet conversation with Oliver, in German, and there were no seats free, so Hal went and sat on the floor beside Freya. As he sank down next to her, he inhaled a heady waft of oranges and geraniums.

'What's that smell?' he asked.

'My perfume,' Freya replied. 'You like it?'

'Yes.' Hal nodded. 'What's your cat's name?'

'Belladonna. It means *beautiful lady*, and she certainly thinks she is one.'

Hal scratched Belladonna under the chin. She turned her amber eyes towards him, half closing them with pleasure. 'Doesn't she mind being on a train?'

88

'Belladonna doesn't like to be left behind. She comes with me everywhere.'

'Isn't belladonna –' Hal eyed Freya suspiciously – 'another name for deadly nightshade?'

'Very good, Harrison.' Freya looked delighted. 'Are you a botanist?'

'No, I saw it on a TV show,' Hal admitted. 'Deadly nightshade is a dangerous poison.'

'*Ja*, it can kill you.' Freya nodded, then leaned forward conspiratorially. 'Did you know it's also an important ingredient in the potion used by witches to help them fly?' She arched an eyebrow and gave a throaty laugh. The cat flinched. 'Oh, *liebling*, did I startle you?' she purred, stroking Belladonna.

Hal stared at Freya, and Rada let out a *pshaww!* and shook her head. 'She likes to tease.' Her sonorous voice was affectionate. 'Take no notice.'

'Me? Tease?' Freya put her hand to her chest and opened her mouth in mock shock.

Hal laughed, and her humorous nature emboldened him to ask the question he really wanted to know the answer to.

'Why is everyone so surprised to see you here?'

Freya dropped her hand and her mouth snapped shut.

'I-I mean,' Hal stammered, realizing he'd asked a sensitive question, 'it's not strange that you should want to go to your brother's funeral.'

After a long pause, Freya answered.

'I grew up in Schloss Kratzenstein. It's my home.' She

looked away, remembering a different time. 'Twenty-eight years ago, when my little brother Manfred died, my mother's grief ate her up from the inside. She died four years later. My father became controlling. Alexander tried to please him by throwing himself into the family business and marrying the woman my parents thought would make a good match for him.'

'Arnie's mother?'

'Bertha.' Freya nodded.

'Alexander was trying to be two sons.' She sighed. 'But every choice I have ever made about my life upsets Papa. I am not interested in the railway. I like plants – I wanted to be a botanist.' She paused. 'And I wasn't interested in marrying the men he introduced me to.' She reached up, taking Rada's hand. 'One day, I'd had enough of hiding who I was, and I told my father that I was going to follow my heart.' She looked down. 'And he told me to leave and never return.' After a long pause, she looked into Hal's eyes. 'And so, I haven't.'

Hal was shocked.

'But now –' Freya stroked Belladonna – 'I think it's time to come home.'

'Does he know you're coming?'

'No.' She swallowed, and Hal saw that she was nervous. 'But it was Papa who wrote to me and told me that Alexander had died, so I hope he will be pleased to see me. After all, I'm his last living child.'

CHAPTER TWELVE

KRATZENSTEIN HALT

'Enough of my troubles,' Freya declared. 'Go and finish your exploration of the train.' She nodded at the door into the next carriage. 'There's a hot-drinks machine in the kitchen.'

Hal got up, tugging Ozan's sleeve, and the boys crossed the veranda to the third carriage. They were standing in a silver-and-blue kitchenette. Hal opened a door in the middle of the carriage and found a compact bathroom with a shower. At the end was the guard's room, where their luggage was stored.

'Want a drink?' Ozan asked, hitting a button on the fancy coffee machine.

'Hot chocolate, please,' Hal answered. 'Did you hear what Freya said about her dad?'

'A bit.' Ozan sounded disinterested. 'Hey, look, it's Magdeburg.' He pointed out of the window as the train crawled through the station. 'We're more than halfway there now.' He opened cupboards until he found cups. 'I wonder if we'll be allowed to play with the model trains. Opa says Arnold Kratzenstein's been building the railway since he was a boy and they run all through the house.'

'You like model railways?'

Ozan thought before answering. 'I like models. It's not about the trains. Small worlds made to a scale are cool.' They went and sat in the booth opposite. 'Once, I made this house for Hilda's dolls, with furniture and everything. I drew the plans to match the scale of her dolls, and constructed the whole thing from boxes.' He looked out of the window. 'If old Arnold is kind, he might let us add to his model railway. I could build him a bridge. That would be fun.'

The ominous dragging in Hal's stomach warned him the weekend was going to be anything but fun. Up ahead, opaque clouds huddled low over distant dark peaks. 'Is that . . .'

'The Harz mountains.' Ozan nodded.

'What do you make of Arnie's curse story?'

'Father told us about the Kratzenstein curse before we came.'

'Does he believe in it?'

'No.' Ozan chuckled. 'He told us to try and make coming to this funeral sound exciting. Hilda loves ghost stories. He told her the old house was haunted by all the ghosts of the cursed sons who'd died.' He snorted.

'You didn't want to come?'

Ozan looked wryly at him. 'Who wants to go to the funeral of a relative they hardly know when it's the holidays?'

'Good point.'

'Mama is away working in Istanbul, so for Papa to come he had to persuade us to agree. He's desperate to see the library.'

'Is it a good one?'

'The Kratzenstein family can be traced back to the Middle Ages, so the library is full of rare old books, but because it is a private house no one can read them.'

'Your dad came to see the rare books?'

'He's crazy about this old dead writer called Goethe. He thinks Goethe may have stayed at Schloss Kratzenstein when he was writing *Faust*. That's why he wants to see the library.'

'*Faust!* My unc— my dad bought that book in Paris.' Hal cursed inwardly at his clumsy speech.

'It's boring.' Ozan pulled a face. 'But it does have witches in it. They all come to the Brocken mountain to have a big evil party with the devil.'

Hal stared out at the shadowy Harz mountains as they crept closer. He noticed the largest one had a flat bald peak, though its side was dark with evergreen trees, and guessed it was the Brocken. He strained his eyes, and thought he could see, at the summit, a blinking light. 'Can you see a red light, up there, on the top of that mountain?'

'That's the old Soviet listening post. The Russians used it during the Cold War to broadcast secret messages.'

Hal stared at the light, transfixed; its flashing was hypnotic. 'Have you met Arnold Kratzenstein?'

'No, but Opa likes him. He knew him before he met Oma. I think it was Arnold who introduced them.'

'They are good friends?'

'It was Arnold who asked Opa to come when Alexander died.'

Suppressing his instinct to draw was creating a traffic jam of thoughts and questions in Hal's head, and he wished he could talk to Uncle Nat about everything that was going on. Why had no one mentioned Alexander Kratzenstein's terrified appearance yet? Perhaps that's what the adults had been talking about when he and Ozan had entered their carriage. Were they keeping it a secret so as not to horrify the children?

The train slowed right down as it approached Wernigerode and stopped at a red signal. Two giant black-and-red steam engines were sitting in a parallel siding, smoke bubbling from their chimneys and Hal gawped, his heart lifting at the sight of the beautiful locomotives.

'That's the Brockenbahn,' Ozan said. 'The steam railway that goes through the mountains. You really like trains, don't you?'

'Yup.' Hal smiled. 'Must be my Kratzenstein DNA.'

'Then be careful the curse doesn't get you!' Ozan said in a ghostly voice, and they laughed.

'Shall we take Herman and Hilda a hot chocolate?' Hal suggested.

'Good idea.' Ozan jumped up, keen to use the drinks machine again. 'We'd better be quick. We'll be there soon.'

It was a mission to carry the hot drinks across the outdoor verandas, but the train was stationary and the grateful smiles from Herman and Hilda made up for the effort.

'Herman is annoyingly good at chess,' Hilda said, sipping

her chocolate. 'This is our third game. He's beaten me twice.'

Herman blushed with pleasure.

The signal changed and the train rolled forward. Hal was delighted to see cobbled streets and wonky old houses out of the window. Travelling through Wernigerode was like going back in time. The buildings were colourful – mustard, coral and yellow – with criss-cross beams and short wooden doors. They looked like fairytale buildings. He pictured Hansel and Gretel coming out of one, scattering breadcrumbs behind them, on their way to the woods, then gave an involuntary shiver as he remembered that they had met a witch in the woods who'd tried to eat them.

Beyond the town was a river, banked by boulders, then came bigger houses, with large gardens. The overhead power cables were gone, and Hal realized the locomotive must have switched to diesel power at the red signal.

'There it is.' Herman pointed up the mountain at a building Hal would have called a castle. 'Schloss Kratzenstein.'

As the train climbed, winding through the foothills of the Brocken, the dense clouds hiding the sky seemed to grow heavier and sink lower. The front of the forbidding manor was a crenellated stone wall with arched windows. In the middle protruded a stubby square porch. Hal guessed this was the main entrance. To the right, a building like the town houses, with criss-cross beams, sprouted forward, as if added as an afterthought. Behind this stern aspect was an enormous tower, a turret on each of its four corners, each with two vertical windows, like vacant black eyes, topped by a conical roof.

95

The closer they got, the more sinister the place seemed.

The rails crossed the drive, taking the train out and round the right side of the building, where there was a glasshouse extension. Then he spotted the archway and a sign: *Kratzenstein Halt*.

'Where do we stop?' Hal asked.

'Inside,' replied Herman as the train went into a tunnel through the walls of the house.

CHAPTER THIRTEEN

A MATTER OF
WIFE AND DEATH

Through the carriage window Hal saw a cobbled courtyard with a short platform protruding from the back of the house. Waiting on it was an old man whose silver hair stuck out like a mad scientist's. Old Arnold Kratzenstein was sitting in a wheelchair with a blanket over his legs. Standing behind the chair, a candyfloss-pink cardigan over her white blouse, was his nurse, Connie, whose crop of blonde hair was neatly pinned up. Beside them, dressed in a black suit jacket and skirt, stood a hard-faced woman with a monobrow. Her frog-like eyes bulged as she scanned the train with pursed lips.

The train stopped, and Arnie jumped down from the loco, bounding over to the woman in black. Her arms shot out and she hugged him, confirming Hal's guess that this was Bertha, Alexander's first wife. He saw Arnie whisper something to his mother and she stiffened.

'You have a station in your house?' Ozan marvelled.

'This is not my house,' Herman muttered.

Uncle Nat and Clara entered the compartment.

'Everyone OK?' Uncle Nat asked. 'Ready to go?'

Clara put her arm protectively round Herman's shoulders and they got off the train. Old Arnold kissed Clara's hand, and then pulled a euro coin from behind Herman's ear, handing it to him with a smile. Uncle Nat stepped forward and, speaking

in German, shook Arnold's hand, offering his condolences and introducing himself and Hal as Nat and Harrison Strom.

Freya was the last to step down from the train, and her appearance shocked the mischief out of old Arnold's eyes. Clutching Belladonna's cat basket and Rada's hand, she smiled nervously. 'Hallo, Papa.'

Arnold opened his mouth to reply, but nothing came out. He studied his daughter's face.

Tactfully the baron suggested to Bertha that they all go inside and, pivoting on her heel, Bertha barked, '*Folgt mir!*'

As they traipsed into the house after Bertha, Hal noticed Connie looking perplexed. She had stepped back from the wheelchair and was staring at Uncle Nat, then she looked at Freya. She didn't know whether to stay with Arnold or follow them into the house.

The salon was a large sage-green room with heavy gold curtains, a high ceiling and a roaring fire in a giant stone hearth. Its walls were decorated with a display of crossbows and criss-crossed spears. Bertha turned, pushing open a pair of double doors framed by an impressively tusked wild boar – stuffed and mounted on a wooden pedestal – on one side, and a suit of armour on the other.

The table in the centre of the panelled dining room was big enough for a Viking banquet. Bertha moved the place settings and added chairs to accommodate the two unexpected guests.

Freya wheeled her father to the head of the table and sat beside him. Bending down, she released Belladonna from her basket and lifted her on to her lap. Bertha had moved

Clara and Herman away from the head of the table and Hal could tell from Clara's expression that she was not impressed. When he got to the chair in front of the *Harrison Strom* place card, he noticed miniature railway tracks running in a loop round the table. He looked about, wondering where the trains were.

'Before we eat . . .' Arnold said as everyone settled into their seats, 'I would like to thank you all for making the journey to be here.' He looked around the table, meeting everyone's eyes. 'This is a tragic time for our family –' he took Freya's and Bertha's hands – 'but we have each other and together we will honour Alexander's life.'

Bertha frowned, biting her lip as she tried to control her emotions, then she barked out a command, in German, making Hal jump. A timid woman hurried in, carrying plates that each held a knuckle of pork, with a knife stabbed into it, and a potato-sized dumpling sitting in the meat juices, accompanied by shredded cabbage.

'*Schweinshaxe* is my favourite.' Uncle Nat smiled at Bertha as the plates were set down. 'This looks delicious.'

'The potato dumpling is a family recipe,' Bertha said with pride.

A high-pitched *toot-toot!* sounded, and a model train made its entrance through a hole in the wall above the door. It circumnavigated the room on a set of rails built on the architrave, carrying in its trucks a selection of mustards, seasonings and sauces; a dish of butter sat in a hopper at the back. The diners looked up, following its journey to a junction, where it paused as the section of the track on which it sat was lowered down on wires, slotting into a groove in the table.

'That is cool,' Ozan murmured.

The train tooted, and moved off slowly, over a set of points, on to the loop of track round the table.

'Please, help yourself,' Arnold said, delighted by the astonishment on his guests' faces.

'Oh, Papa,' Freya said affectionately. 'You haven't changed.'

Pulling out the knife, Hal tucked in. The meat was tender, the crackling salty and crunchy.

Like a sponge, the dumpling soaked up the juices, and the sauerkraut, flavoured with salt, vinegar and rye seeds, went with it well. He was so hungry that he didn't notice an argument start at the other end of the table.

Clara and Bertha were speaking to each other in stiff, hushed German and, although he didn't understand what they were saying, their loathing for one another was obvious. Other conversations petered out as everyone around the table became aware of the exchange.

Bertha switched to English. 'People from the city are so difficult to please,' she said pointedly. Her left nostril twitched as if she were suppressing a sneer.

'But we always stay in Alexander's rooms,' Clara replied, looking distressed. 'I am his wife . . .'

'Connie is with us now.' Without taking her eyes from Clara, Bertha tipped her head towards Connie, who was sitting at the foot of the table, beside Aksel. 'She has Manfred's old room,' Bertha continued, 'because she must be close to Arnold. He needs her. My Arnie's bedroom is Freya's old room.' She smiled sourly at Freya. 'If Freya is to be near her father, she must stay in Alexander's rooms.'

'Oh!' Freya looked distressed. 'Rada and I don't mind where we stay. We know we weren't expected.'

'*Schatz*,' Arnold said tenderly, putting his liver-spotted hand on Freya's. 'It's been twenty years. You will stay in the family rooms.'

'I too was Alexander's wife,' Bertha said. 'My rooms are in the servants' quarters. The blue room is our finest guest room.'

She paused, her expression triumphant. 'Is it not good enough for you?'

'It's on the other side of the house.' Clara looked at Bertha with stone-cold hatred. 'Herman and I will be away from the family. It was him I was concerned about.'

'You must not worry about Herman,' Bertha replied. 'All the children will stay together in the tower.'

'*Nein*,' Clara said through gritted teeth. 'Herman stays with me.'

'Wouldn't Herman rather be with his cousins?' There was a mean glint in Bertha's eyes. 'Playing will be a healthy distraction from . . . tragic events. Don't you think?'

Clara frowned and turned to Herman. 'Would you rather sleep in the tower with your cousins?'

Herman glanced nervously at Hal and said in a barely audible whisper, 'It would be nice to be with my cousins.'

Clara looked crestfallen, but nodded.

'It is not an easy task to accommodate so many people, so . . . suddenly.' Bertha's voice cracked, and she cleared her throat, dabbing her napkin to her eyes. 'I have done my best.'

'You have done well, Bertha,' the baron reassured her. 'And you have fed us a comforting meal.' There were murmurs of agreement, but Clara pushed her lips together so hard that they went white. Hal looked across the table at Hilda and Ozan. They appeared to be as excited as he was about sleeping in the tower. 'Tomorrow,' the baron continued, 'I understand, we will be able to pay our respects?'

Bertha nodded. 'Tomorrow Alexander will be laid in the funeral carriage in the halt.' Her bottom lip wobbled, and she clenched her jaw to steady her emotions. 'Tomorrow there will be time for each of you to pay your last respects and say goodbye.'

CHAPTER FOURTEEN

KINDERTURM

After lunch they filed back into the salon and Hal took the opportunity to lift the helmet visor of the suit of armour and peek inside.

'Arnie.' Bertha signalled for him to come to her and spoke softly. '*Die Feuer wurden alle angezündet, um die Hexe fernzuhalten. Lass sie nicht raus.*'

'Did you hear that?' Hilda whispered to Hal and Ozan. 'Bertha told Arnie that all the fires have been lit to keep away the witch.' Her dark eyes danced. 'She believes in the curse!'

Hal looked at the flames licking the logs in the hearth. Curse or no curse, he was glad the fires were blazing. It was cold in the mountains.

'Arnie will take the children to the tower now,' Bertha announced, 'and I will take you to your rooms.'

'Bertha, I want to show Rada the house,' Freya said, approaching her. 'Don't worry about our bags. We'll make our own way to our room. I know where it is.'

Bertha's expression darkened as Freya spoke. She didn't like deviations from her plan. 'Why are you here, Freya?' she asked in a low, clipped voice. 'You didn't go to either of Alexander's weddings – why attend his funeral?' She raised her eyebrows. 'Perhaps you are happy he's dead?'

'Oh, Bertha, you're so sweet,' Freya mocked. 'It's such a mystery to me why Alexander left you and ran away to Berlin.' She swirled away, grabbing Rada by the hand. 'Come, Rada. I'm going to show you the orangery.'

Arnie called the children. 'Right, you *Kotzbrocken*. This way to the *Kinderturm*.'

'What's *Kinderturm*?' Hal asked Hilda.

'Children's tower.'

Arnie marched them back through the dining room and out of a door on the other side into a hall. 'Those stairs go to the first floor – Opa's rooms and the family bedrooms. From there, another staircase takes you up the tower.' He pressed a button in the wall. It lit up. 'Or there's Opa's elevator.'

They filed into the lift. With all their bags, it was a tight squeeze, but after some wriggling they got the gate shut. When the door opened, they were in a freezing stone hallway. To the right was a staircase down, in front of them an oak door. Arnie twisted the iron ring door handle and a wave of heat washed over them as the door opened and they surged into the square room. Everyone began talking at once.

'Oh, a nice warm fire!' Hilda pointed at the merry blaze, giving Hal a meaningful look.

'This is my bed,' Ozan called out, running to a set of bunk beds on the far side of the room and leaping up on to the top one.

'I take this one,' Hilda said, bellyflopping on a double bed covered by a patchwork quilt, beside a bookcase.

'Where would you like to sleep?' Hal asked Herman.

Herman hesitated, then pointed to the bunk below Ozan, which meant the single bed closest to the fireplace was Hal's.

'What's up there?' Hal asked Arnie, pointing at a spiral staircase that corkscrewed into the roof.

'TV and video games.'

Hal looked at Ozan, and they scrambled for the stairs.

'You break anything,' Arnie called at their backs, 'you pay for it.'

Emerging under the pointed roof of the tower, Hal saw three beanbag chairs strewn across the floor in front of a dusty TV hooked up to an old console. Battered books, jigsaws and board games lined the low shelves around the edges of the room. On the top were model railway tracks.

'Look! Arnold's railway comes all the way up here,' Hal exclaimed, but Ozan had turned on the games console and Herman was dragging a beanbag over, talking excitedly in German. It was cold away from the fire. Above his head, the shadowy recess of the tower was hung with cobwebs and Hal was puzzled by the black lumps he could see attached to the beams.

The window in the attic room was mostly obscured by a model of beautifully rendered mountainside, with rocks, trees, shrubs. A tunnel passed through it for the model railway that ran off the bookcase into the deep ledge. Interested to see how it had been constructed, Hal peered over the top and down the gap between it and the glass. He was surprised to see a red

109

railway signal lantern embedded in the Styrofoam, facing the window.

Kneeling down, Hal examined the model and discovered a switch inside the tunnel. Taking his pen from his pocket, he poked it into the tunnel and flicked the switch. The red lantern went on. Hal grinned, pleased to have worked it out.

Turning it off, he turned to tell Ozan and Herman, but they were intently playing a fighting game, so he went back downstairs. Hilda was curled up on her bed with her book.

'Where's Arnie?'

'Gone,' Hilda replied without looking up. 'If you need it, the bathroom is there.' She pointed to a door behind the spiral staircase.

'Don't you want to see upstairs?'

'No.' She looked up. 'Arnie says there are bats hibernating in the tower. They have their own tiny door to come in and out of.' She shuddered. 'I don't like bats.' She lifted the book. 'And I'm at a good bit in my story. The children of Berlin have become detectives to help Emil find the man who stole his money on the train.'

Hal took a tour of the four turrets, looking out of each of the windows to orientate himself. His eyes followed the track through the courtyard out the other side. It passed a pair of train sheds, he spotted the points, then it curved away up towards the mountain. He gasped.

'What is it?' Hilda asked.

'Dead Man's Pass,' he whispered.

Hilda came to his side. 'Is that where Arnie saw the witch?'

'It's where Alexander died . . .'

'. . . of a heart attack . . .'

'. . . with a twisted look of terror on his face.'

'What?'

Hal's stomach lurched as he looked into Hilda's dark, questioning eyes. He'd slipped up. The others didn't know about the mysterious details of Alexander's death. 'You mustn't tell Herman,' he whispered, in a panic. 'I shouldn't have said anything. I'm sorry if it gives you nightmares . . . I . . .'

'Nightmares?' Hilda said scornfully. 'I'm not six! Why did he look terrified?'

'You must swear not to tell.'

'I swear.' Hilda crossed her fingers over her heart. 'Was he killed by the witch?'

'The adults think he was frightened to death.'

'Really?' Hilda looked thrilled. 'How do you know about it?'

Unable to think of a better lie, Hal blurted out, 'I listen at doorways!'

'Me too!' Hilda grinned. 'You have to if you're going to be a detective.'

'A detective?'

'Yes. When I grow up, I'm going to be a detective. I love reading about mysteries because I can never find real ones to solve. Maybe this is a real mystery.' She looked thrilled.

Hal wanted to tell her that he *was* a detective and working the case already, but he knew he couldn't. Worried that something might slip out if they kept talking, and keen to be alone with his uncle and have the talk he'd promised, he said, 'I've got to go downstairs and find my dad.'

'Keep your eyes peeled for clues,' Hilda said, going back to her bed and her book, 'and I'll do the same.'

Hal stuffed his pocketbook and pen into his trouser pocket. Looking for clues was exactly what he planned to do on his way to find Uncle Nat.

Arnie had taken the lift, so Hal took the stairs. He came out on the carpeted landing of the first floor, and through an open door saw Arnie in a messy bedroom bobbing his head to loud rock music. These were the family rooms where Clara had wanted to stay. They were laid out around the base of

112

the tower. Hal thought if he was going to search the house for clues he should draw a floor plan, so he pulled out his pocketbook and pen.

Hearing a buzzing *tickety-tack*, he looked up at a model passenger train running above his head on the architrave. Spurred on by the joy of the thing, he followed the train until it disappeared through a tunnel in the wall beside a door. Without thinking, he pushed the door open and found himself in a small-scale railway wonderland.

Tiny tracks wove across a maze of landscaped tables, linked by tunnels and bridges. A dozen model trains whirred around them. From a rolling field, miniature children waved at a steam engine passing a level crossing, while yellow U-Bahn carriages rattled on stilts above a model city. Workmen rested on the fence of a quarry, while a diesel engine pulled a string of hoppers filled with miniscule rocks. In a siding, Hal spied the train of condiments from dinner. It was beside a tunnel built up over a hole in the floor and he realized this room was directly above the dining room.

'Pleasing, isn't it?' Arnold said.

Hal jumped. He hadn't heard the door behind him open, or Arnold's wheelchair roll in. 'I'm sorry, sir,' he blurted out, realizing he'd strayed into the old man's private rooms. 'I didn't mean—'

'Don't be.' Arnold chuckled. 'You're the first to find this room. You must have an adventurous spirit.' He considered Hal. 'You like trains?' Hal nodded. 'Of course you do.'

'Arnold, are you playing with your trains again,' came the

softly chiding voice of Connie. The nurse smiled brightly as she came into the room, and held out her hand to Hal. 'Forgive me, I've forgotten your name. I'm Connie Müller.'

Hal shook her hand. 'Harrison Strom.'

'Pleased to meet you, Harrison Strom. I hope you don't mind, but it's Arnold's nap time and it's my job to see that he takes it.' She leaned forward. 'He's a terrible grouch if he doesn't get a nap.'

'Give me five minutes with Harrison,' Arnold said. 'Then I'll come.'

'I'm relying on you, Harrison,' Connie said with a wink. 'Once Arnold starts talking about trains, he can go on for hours.'

Hal grinned. 'We won't be long.'

'Come and take a closer look,' Arnold said, wheeling himself to a passage between the table and the window. 'This is my favourite place. From here I can see my trains, big and small.' He pointed to the window and the table. 'This room is where Schloss Kratzenstein's model rail services start and end.'

Hal came to stand beside him and looked out of the window. The Bombardier TRAXX locomotive had gone, and Aksel was on his back with his head under one of the carriages.

'What's Aksel doing?'

'Uncoupling the carriages. The track up the Brocken has a narrow gauge, so he will shunt them to the train sheds to change their bogies. On Monday, our Class 99 – a vintage tank engine – will pull the funeral train up the mountain. She's been in the family for over a hundred years.' He sighed and after a long silence, said, 'It's a terrible thing to outlive your sons.'

Hal wanted to say something kind. 'I'm sorry,' was all he could think of.

'Me too.' Arnold nodded sadly, staring past him at Dead Man's Pass. 'It was me she wanted,' he muttered with a tiny shake of his head.

'Who wanted?' Hal asked in a whisper.

Arnold blinked, and then forced a smile. 'Aksel will show you the steam engine if you ask him. His English isn't good, but he can understand what you're saying.' He turned his chair round. 'I must go, or Connie will come and scold us. Enjoy the house and the trains, Harrison. Don't let the grown-ups prevent you from having fun.' He rolled through the doorway, then looked back over his shoulder, and said, 'See if you can make Herman smile, will you?'

The door closed, and Hal stood rooted to the spot, only the fizzing, clicking sound of trains audible as Arnold's words echoed in his head. *It was me she wanted . . .*

Was he talking about the witch?

CHAPTER FIFTEEN

A BATTLE OF WILLS

Connie had seen the witch, Bertha was scared of the witch and Arnold thought she'd come for him. Did everyone in Schloss Kratzenstein believe in her curse?

Marking Arnold's room of model trains on his plan, Hal left by the opposite door, and found himself in a hallway. He wasn't sure of the way to the guest rooms, but it occurred to him that a snoop about might be a good way of uncovering a clue.

Looking through a doorway to his left, Hal saw a thin corridor with three rooms branching off it. Checking no one was coming, he darted down it. The first was a bathroom; the second was a fastidiously neat bedroom with only a hairbrush and a pot of Nivea face cream on the dressing table. A silver-framed family photograph was on the bedside table. He stepped inside to get a closer look and immediately realized whose room this was. His heart thumped against his ribs, warning him not to get caught. The picture was of a younger Bertha smiling up at Alexander; he was looking at her lovingly, and between them was little Arnie, holding their hands. In the picture, Bertha looked happy and pretty.

The third room was a characterless sitting room, with a sofa, a TV as old as the one in the tower and a sideboard with a coffee machine and two cups, one containing little packets of sugar. There were no books or magazines, but beneath the window was a narrow desk. One of the drawers had been closed in a hurry because a triangle of paper was poking out.

Taking a step towards the desk, Hal froze as the distant *click-clack* of heeled shoes announced he was about to be caught. Leaping backwards, he hurried to the end of the corridor, and found himself face to face with Bertha.

'What do you think you are doing?' she demanded.

'Oh, thank goodness, Mrs Kratzenstein,' Hal spluttered. 'I'm looking for my dad's room, but I'm lost!'

Bertha's expression relaxed, but she didn't smile. 'Your father's room is that way.' She pointed behind her. 'At the end. Third door on the right.' She paused. 'Harrison Strom . . .'

'Yes?' Hal's heart was thumping.

'I know why your father is here.' She leaned forward, so the tip of her nose was barely an inch from his face. 'And it is not to pay his respects to my Alexander.'

Hal stared into the angry face of Bertha Kratzenstein, trying to think of something to say.

'You tell him I know what he wants to get his hands on, and he's not going to get it.' She pushed past him, going into her sitting room and closing the door.

Hal wondered what Bertha could have meant by her

strange warning. Did she know who they really were? He didn't think so, but she seemed to think Uncle Nat had an underhand motive for being here. She was suspicious of everyone. She didn't like Freya or Clara, and he wondered if it was because they threatened her position as the housekeeper of Schloss Kratzenstein.

An ornate wooden arch signified the entrance to the guest bedrooms. Hal knocked at the door Bertha had said belonged to Uncle Nat, but there was no reply. Feeling frustrated, he tried the handle and the door opened.

Uncle Nat's holdall was on the bed, unzipped, his things scattered on the counterpane. Hal went in and picked up the copy of *Faust* they'd bought in Paris, opened it to a page where a piece of paper had been inserted, and saw that Uncle Nat had made a mark next to some lines of the play.

> *Up Brocken mountain witches fly,*
> *When stubble is yellow and green the crop.*
> *Gathering on Walpurgis night,*
> *Carrying Lucifer aloft.*
> *Over stream and fern, gorse and ditch,*
> *Tramp stinking goat and farting witch.*

Hal snorted. What kind of play *was* this?

The piece of paper he was holding was covered in scribbled letters and numbers, as if Uncle Nat had been working out a crossword clue, but they didn't make any sense to Hal, so he returned it to the page and put the book back on the bed.

When he knocked at the next door, it was opened by Alma Essenbach.

'Hello, Harrison.' She looked over his shoulder, expecting her grandchildren to be with him. 'Are Ozan and Hilda behaving themselves?'

'They're in the tower.' Hal nodded. 'Ozan is playing video games with Herman, and Hilda is reading. I was looking for my . . .' He blushed, remembering that Alma knew the truth about who he was and what he was doing. 'Uncle.'

'He's in the study with Wolfgang and Oliver.'

'Where's that?'

'At the front of the house,' Alma said, glancing at his pocketbook. 'Are you investigating? Can I help?'

'I'm mapping the house.' Hal pointed to the opposite door. 'Whose room is that?'

'Oliver's. Clara's room is at the front of the house beside the study.'

'Why is Clara upset about having the front room?'

'Clara has always stayed in the family's part of the house with Alexander. Now that he's gone, Bertha has used Freya's sudden arrival to put her in the formal side of the house. It's like saying she's no longer a part of the family.' Alma shook her head. 'Bertha is jealous of Clara, because Alexander fell in love with her.'

'If Bertha and Alexander are divorced, why does she still live here?'

'She and Alexander were matched by their parents when they were teenagers. They married young, lived here and had

119

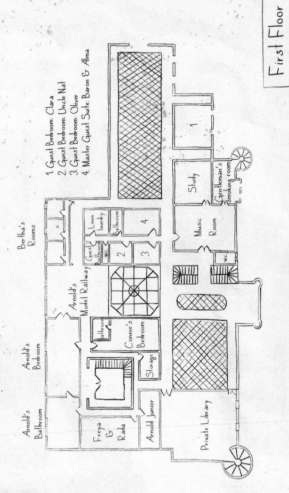

Schloss Kratzenstein

First Floor

1 Guest Bedroom: Clara
2 Guest Bedroom: Uncle Nat
3 Guest Bedroom: Oliver
4 Master Guest Suite: Baron & Alma

Bertha's Rooms

Arnold's Model Railway

Arnold's Bedroom

Arnold's Ballroom

Freya & Rada

Arnold Junior

Private Library

Connie's Bedroom

Storage

Guest Bathroom WC

Linen

Laundry

Bathroom

Music Room

Study

Gentleman's Smoking Room

WC

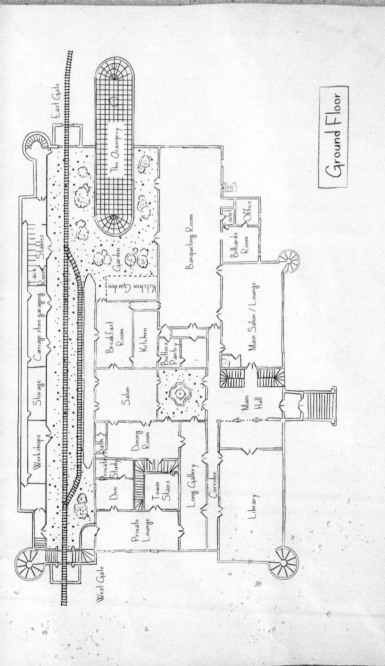

Ground Floor

East Gate

West Gate

The Orangery

Garden

Kitchen Garden

Back Room

Stables

Carriage store / garaging Room

Storage

Workshops

Breakfast Room

Kitchen

Butler's Pantry

Salon

Private Bath

Dining Room

Den / Study

Tower Stairs

Private Lounge

Long Gallery

Corridor

Library

Banqueting Room

Billiards Room

Toilet

Office

Main Salon / Lounge

Main Hall

Arnie. As their marriage fell apart, Alexander spent more and more time in Berlin until one day he announced he was going to live there and that he was in love with Clara. Bertha was devastated. She loved Alexander and still does. Arnold took pity on her and said she could stay living here with Arnie. I think Alexander expected Bertha would leave once Arnie turned eighteen, but when the old housekeeper died, Bertha took on her role, to earn her keep, and Arnold agreed she could stay permanently. It was a cause of argument between Alexander and his father. But Arnold said Bertha took care of him, as well as her being the mother of his grandson, and he wouldn't hear of her leaving if she didn't want to.' She paused. 'I think that's why Alexander hired Connie.'

'Alexander hired Connie?'

Alma nodded. 'To show Bertha wasn't needed.'

'Oh!' Hal felt sorry for Bertha. He thought of the framed family photograph. 'Alma, when Arnie frightened us with his story at the dinner table yesterday, he said something about a skull face in Dead Man's Pass. What was he talking about?'

'The rock face at the entrance to the pass has the features of a skull. The story is that when the Kratzenstein's blew their way through the mountain to make a cutting for their private railway the skull was revealed as a sign that the family was cursed.'

'Oh!'

'You can't miss it if you're going into the pass.'

'Thanks. I'd better get on with my investigation. I need to speak to Uncle Nat. How do I get to the study?'

Alma pointed down the corridor. 'Go left at the end. You'll find yourself in the gallery above the Banqueting Hall. Walk past the double doors – the study is the next room.'

Hal thanked her and hurried away. The shadows in the old house had grown longer throughout the afternoon, and there were more dark corners now than when he'd first arrived. He sped up, racing round the corner, and yelped as he came face to face with a giant, amber-eyed wolf.

The wolf was stuffed and mounted on a wooden plinth with a metal plaque at its feet that read: *Adalwolf* (*Canis lupus*). It was positioned so it was looking straight at anyone coming down the corridor and had one paw lifted and teeth bared. Hal had never seen a wolf before. It was large, its unblinking stare unnerving.

From the gallery, he looked down into a vast banqueting hall big enough to race remote control cars around it. The curtains were closed and dust sheets covered the paintings. Hearing the muffled sound of voices, he tip-toed to the study door and put his ear to it.

ADALWOLF, CANIS LUPUS.
Taxidermy wolf.

'That is *not* Alexander's will,' Clara was saying angrily. 'He replaced his first will when he replaced his first wife.'

'You've seen the second will?' It was the baron's voice.

'Of course. Alexander rewrote his will after Herman was born.'

'Did he make a copy?'

'Why would he make a copy? He kept it locked in the family safe.'

'This was the only will in the safe,' Uncle Nat said.

'But that's not his will!' There was a note of hysteria in Clara's voice.

'I'm sure there's an explanation.' The baron was trying to soothe her.

'Yes. Yes, there is.' Clara drew in gulps of air trying not to cry. 'That *herrschsüchtige Frau*. She's taken his will. Bertha cares more about being a Kratzenstein than she did about being Alexander's wife. She's trying to . . .' She hiccupped and burst into tears. Hal heard shushing noises and the movement of furniture.

Thinking back to the corner of paper he'd seen poking out of Bertha's desk, Hal chided himself for not being more decisive when he'd had the opportunity to look. Could that have been Alexander's will?

Something brushed up against his leg and Hal went rigid, fearing he'd been caught, but it was Belladonna. The black cat made a figure of eight through his legs, purring noisily. Backing away from the study door, Hal silently shushed the cat, picking her up. The double doors to the next room were

124

ajar, so he peeped in. He saw a grand piano and guessed it was a music room. Belladonna struggled in his arms, landing on the ground with a thud. Fearing the cat would get him caught, he stepped into the dark room and grabbed for her, but she disappeared into the shadows.

'Harrison?' There was a woman silhouetted in the doorway and Hal opened his mouth to cry out, but she stepped back and the Banqueting Hall light revealed it was Connie. She put her finger to her lips and took Hal's arm, pulling him back towards the gallery. 'I wouldn't go in there if I were you. Arnold asked me to come and give Baron Essenbach a message, but Clara is angry about the missing will and I dare not intrude.'

Hal gladly walked with her. He had a question he'd been itching to ask Connie since he'd arrived. 'Arnie says you saw the witch.'

Connie closed her cardigan across her body, hugging her arms around herself as if suddenly cold. 'I don't know who I saw.'

'But you saw someone?'

Connie nodded, looking unhappy.

'What did she look like?'

'I was coming back from a walk and lost my way on the mountain. Ice mists appear fast here. It's the climate.' Her eyes flickered to a window, as if she could see through the closed curtains. 'I wandered into a clearing and was startled to see a dead rat cut open on a boulder, its guts all pulled out.' Her face screwed up in disgust. 'There was a woman standing behind it. She wore a grey hood. Her eyes were as black as night, her cloak the colour of the mist.' Connie stopped walking.

'And?' Hal prompted.

Connie looked at him, haunted by the memory. 'She vanished. Right in front of me. One moment she was standing there, the next, gone. I called out, reaching through the mist, but it was as if my seeing her had dissolved her. I have never been so terrified.'

'What did you do?'

'I ran,' Connie replied with a weak smile. 'I know it's silly. I don't believe in ghosts, and yet I saw one.' She went to the top of a grand staircase. Looking back at him, she said, 'Why did your father bring you here?' She paused for an answer, but Hal was taken aback by the question and didn't reply. 'Tell him you want to go home. This place is cursed. Bad things happen here. I will stay for Mr Kratzenstein's funeral, but not much longer. I don't think it's right to leave when he's the one who hired me, but –' she lowered her voice, glancing about – 'no one ever visits. Bertha and Arnie don't like me being here. The only person I can talk to is Aksel.' She stopped and looked down. Hal noticed she was blushing. 'I'd better get back. Arnold will wake soon.'

CHAPTER SIXTEEN

THE CURSED LIBRARY

Going to the banister, Hal looked down on Connie hurrying away. Hanging below him, on the landing halfway down the sweeping staircase, was a giant portrait of a stern man grasping a walking stick in his right hand. He was standing on top of Dead Man's Pass, railway tracks in the foreground, at his feet, and a cold, swirling mist behind him. An ornate gold plaque at the foot of the frame declared he was Franz Christian Kratzenstein.

Hal wondered if this was the man who'd brought the curse down on the family.

At the foot of the stairs was a grand entrance hall. He decided to explore it. When he reached the landing, he heard the click of a door opening and stopped, holding his breath.

'It's this way,' Herman said.

'This better not be boring,' Ozan muttered. 'I was about to beat your high score.'

'I'm telling you, the library is the best place . . .' Hilda whispered excitedly.

'Best place for what?' Hal asked, smiling as all three of them jumped.

'An investigation,' Hilda replied, recovering herself. 'The library is the best place to start an investigation. We're being detectives.'

Ozan grinned at him. 'What are you doing?'

'Looking for my dad.'

'Didn't you find him?' Hilda asked.

'He's in the study talking with the grown-ups.' Hal shook his head. 'But I did find Arnold's model railway, and a massive stuffed wolf. I almost jumped out of my skin when I saw it!'

Herman giggled. 'Opa put Adalwolf there on purpose, to frighten the guests when they get up to pee in the night. He thinks it's funny.'

'Adalwolf?'

'All the dead animals have names.' Herman pointed under the stairs. 'In that bathroom is Björn the bear. He can give you a shock even if you know he's there.'

'You've seen the model railway?' Ozan asked. 'Where is it?'

'In the room above the dining room. Arnold said we can go and see it whenever we want.'

'You're not allowed to touch the trains,' Herman said. 'They're on timers. Opa controls them from his room.'

'Can we go now?' Ozan asked.

'We're being detectives,' Hilda protested. 'You agreed that we should investigate the curse so we can protect Herman.'

Ozan puffed out his cheeks and Herman blushed. 'OK, but after the library we go and see the trains.' Hal fell into step beside him, and he muttered. 'Don't know what she expects to find in there – it's just a room full of books.'

'It's what's inside the books that interests me,' Hilda said, a note of exasperation in her voice.

The heavy doors creaked open, and the children stepped into a hall of wood and stone leading to a cathedral-like window of clear glass, beneath which stood an enormous antique globe. The innumerable volumes, a heady musk of old paper mixed with furniture polish and deadened sound silenced their chatter. On the left, bookcases of ancient leather-bound books extended into the space, separated by a thin arched window. Access to the highest shelves was via a gallery where there were ladders on rails.

As Hilda walked to the middle of the floor, she slowly turned, her arms open wide, greedily drinking it all in.

Ozan went straight to the giant globe, which was as tall as he was, and spun it.

'There must be thousands of books in here,' Hal whispered.

'Isn't it magnificent?' Hilda said breathlessly, going to a shelf, tilting her head and reading the spines.

Hal followed her, but was dismayed to find that every book was in German. He went to the window. 'It's snowing!' he cried, and the others turned to see. 'Do you think it will settle?'

'It's cold enough,' Ozan said.

'We could build a snowman,' Herman said, and actually smiled.

'Right, where's this secret room, then?' Ozan said, eager to get the trip to the library over with.

'Secret room?' Hal was immediately interested.

'It's where the oldest books are, the precious ones,' Herman said. 'The Kratzenstein commonplace books are kept there. Opa says they are important historical documents about the German railway.'

'What's a commonplace book?' Hal asked.

'I know!' Hilda butted in. 'They're diaries or scrapbooks. We made one as a school project. People used to put everything in their commonplace books – how much money they spent on things for their home, business accounts, recipes, quotations from clever people or poems. Anything that needed to be recorded went into the family commonplace book. And people wrote tiny, because paper was expensive. They drew lines to divide up a page and covered every centimetre of it.'

They followed Herman to a small wooden door in a turret in the corner.

'Do you think the family would have written about the curse?' Hal asked.

'Let's find out,' Ozan said, trying the door handle. 'It's locked!'

In the arched window, beside the door, stood a ferocious-looking stuffed stoat, up on its hind legs, baring its teeth. Herman pulled the stoat's jaw down, and a drawer popped open in the wooden pedestal on which it was standing. Inside the drawer was an iron key.

'Cool,' Hal declared.

Herman unlocked the door to reveal a spiral staircase inside the stone turret. Following him up the stairs, Hal thought they'd find themselves on the gallery, but they emerged in a small room with a square rug, a wooden table in front of a porthole window and walls lined with books – some of them fastened to shelves with black chains.

'How does the library catalogue work?' Hilda asked.

'I don't know,' Herman admitted. 'I come here to get away from everyone. It's quiet, and no one thinks of looking for me here.'

'Which ones are the commonplace books?' Hal asked.

Herman pointed to a bookshelf with volumes the size of atlases, and they crowded round.

'There are dates on the side.' Ozan tipped his head to read them. 'What date are we looking for?'

'I'm not sure,' Hilda said, looking at Herman.

'Wait, everyone, step back!' Hal grabbed their arms. 'Look.' He pointed at the shelf.

'At what?' Ozan asked.

'The dust on the shelf. It's been disturbed.' He pointed to a mark in the dust before an ancient volume. 'Someone has taken out this book recently.'

'It could be a clue.' Hilda carefully slid out the book, taking it to the table and opened the cover. The ink may once have been black, but time had turned it brown and yellowed the paper, which was crowded with the spidery scrawls of a minute German hand, unreadable to Hal.

'*Ich fasse es nicht!*' Hilda exclaimed, looking appalled.

'What's wrong?' asked Hal.

'Some idiot has turned over a corner of a page!'

Ozan snorted. 'So?'

'Don't laugh. This is an important historical document, and very old! This will damage the page.' She unfolded the corner. 'It weakens the paper structure. *It could rip.*'

'Wait.' Hal stopped her. 'What's on that page? Can you read it?'

'The handwriting is so tiny . . .' Hilda squinted, bringing her face close to the paper. Herman opened the table drawer and handed her a magnifying glass. 'Isn't it cool that someone

from hundreds of years ago can communicate with us, right now?'

'They can't communicate with me,' said Hal. 'I don't understand a word of it.'

'Languages are codes,' Hilda said. 'Anyone can read them, but you need the right key.'

'A key?'

'Something to unlock the meaning. You can't understand German, but if you had a phrasebook you would start to understand these words.'

'Cracking a code is more exciting than translating a language,' Ozan said.

'No, it's just easier. I find a complicated puzzle is more satisfying to solve,' Hilda retorted.

Hal thought back to the code word H A N G M A N he'd found hidden in the baron's letter to Uncle Nat. 'What kind of things can be a key to a code?'

'Anything,' Hilda said. 'It could be a number – for example the number seven. This would mean every letter A would be written as a G, because it is seven letters further on in the alphabet. The essential thing, if you're using a code, is that the code maker and the code breaker have the same key . . . Oh! I think I've found something.' Hilda leaned closer. 'It's an account of the day they blew up the rocks to make the railway cutting.'

'Dead Man's Pass?' Hal felt a thrill.

'Here it lists the quantity and the cost of the explosives, and here is a record of the wages they paid the men doing the work. It says they employed fourteen local men, and then there's a line here . . . *May the twenty-sixth. Accident – a rockfall killed a man and injured three. Herr Babelin died.* And then there's an amount of money. I think this was paid to the families as compensation.'

'Is there anything about the curse?' Ozan asked.

Hilda traced her finger along the words without touching the paper. 'There's something here.' She screwed up her face as she read. 'Frau Gobel Babelin refused the compensation. She spoke out publicly against the Kratzensteins, demanding justice for her dead son. The family employed a lawyer. There's a sum of money entered for his fee.' Her eyes scanned to the

134

bottom and over to the adjacent page. 'Franz Kratzenstein's lawyer tries to get Frau Babelin to take the compensation money by threatening her with eviction. Her home is owned by the Meyer family, who are investors in the Kratzenstein railway.' There was a long pause as Hilda read on, her lips half forming the words. 'Here it is. A few days later, Frau Babelin, dressed in black, climbs to the top of Dead Man's Pass and shrieks and wails for hours, cursing the rails, the rocks and the Kratzensteins for taking away her son. No one can get her to come down. In the end, she is dragged away by the village guards, and calls down a curse on the Kratzensteins, that their sons should die unnatural deaths, before their time, like hers did.' She skimmed the rest of the page and drew a breath. 'Oh! Frau Babelin died two days later in the jail. Whoever wrote this entered it as a money saving, because they would no longer need to pay compensation for killing her son.'

The four of them were silent.

'*Ach, nein!*' Hilda whispered, the blood draining from her face.

'What?' Hal asked, dreading the answer.

'They used the rock from the pass to build this library.'

CHAPTER SEVENTEEN

CATS, BATS AND CAULDRONS

'Sons for a son,' Herman whispered, looking at Hilda with wide eyes. 'I will have to pay for what my ancestors did to Frau Babelin and her son.'

Hal shivered, feeling the horror of the curse for the first time.

'Herman, you must not believe in curses.' Hilda put her arm round him in a motherly gesture.

'They're only words,' Ozan said.

'Sticks and stones may break my bones, but words will never hurt me,' Hal said, to reassure himself as well as Herman. 'It's a saying we have in England.'

'Sticks and stones can break your bones, and this curse is going to kill me,' Herman said, his expression grave. 'I heard them talking about how Papa died.'

Hal and Hilda exchanged a look of alarm.

'Heart attacks happen to a lot of people . . .' Ozan started to say, but Herman was shaking his head.

'You don't understand. My father . . . if there were arguments, he always won. He was fearless. I have never seen him nervous or scared, not once, in my whole life.' He paused. 'But Baron Essenbach told my mother that when Papa was found he had the look of a terrified man.'

'Terrified?' Ozan was startled. 'How?'

'I don't know,' Herman admitted. He pointed at the commonplace book. 'It doesn't say in there how Frau Babelin died. What if she did a spell, so her spirit would haunt us till the last son is dead? She is the witch. I know it.'

'Herman, you're scaring yourself,' Hal said softly. 'If the curse were true, your grandfather wouldn't be alive.' But Hal remembered Arnold saying *It was me she wanted*, and found himself wondering if Frau Babelin had killed the wrong Kratzenstein.

'Exactly,' Hilda said brightly. 'Now, Ozan, didn't you say you wanted to see Herman's Opa's model trains? We've learned all we can here. Let's go.' She closed the book and returned it to its shelf.

'Cool! Let's go back to the tower and play video games so I can beat your high score!' Ozan said cheerily to Herman, who replied with a weak smile, and he let them bundle him down the stairs.

'Do you believe in the curse?' Ozan asked Hal on the way down. Hal paused before shaking his head. Ozan lowered his voice so Herman couldn't hear. 'But something must have frightened Alexander Kratzenstein.'

'It could have been a wild animal,' Hal said, thinking of Adalwolf.

Ozan grabbed his arm, 'What if it was *murder*?'

'If it was murder, the adults would have called the police.'

Ozan let go of his sleeve, considering this.

'And if you wanted to murder someone, wouldn't you choose a better way than frightening them to death?'

When they had passed through the library doors, Hal pulled the turret door key from his pocket. 'We forgot to put the key back in the stoat! You go ahead. I'll catch you up.' And he disappeared back into the library, whipping out his pocketbook and pen. Fast as he could, Hal drew the commonplace book on its shelf and the disturbed dust. That book had been pulled out recently, but no others had been touched. The page containing the story of the curse had been marked. Someone had turned over that corner. Hal wanted to know who and why.

After he'd made notes on the content of the commonplace book and replaced the key he'd purposefully pocketed, Hal crossed the grand entrance hall and went through a pair of glass doors and into a courtyard with a fountain in the middle. The basin was dry. Either the water was off or the pipes had frozen. Hal saw with disappointment that there was no snow on the ground. He looked up and was surprised to find the peculiar, cobbled courtyard in the middle of the house had a high domed glass roof, divided into a geometric pattern of leaded triangles. The glass was covered in a thin layer of snow.

There was a high-pitched cry, and a dark shadow padded

138

out from an ivy-clad corner of the courtyard.

'Belladonna!' Hal exclaimed. 'How did you get in here?' She rubbed her nose against his knee. 'Are you lost? Did you get trapped?' He picked the cat up. 'Let's take you back to Freya.'

The opposite doors took him into the green salon with the wild boar and the suit of armour. He took Opa's lift to the first floor, passed Arnold's bedroom and knocked at the next door, hoping it was the right one.

Rada opened it. 'Belladonna!' she exclaimed, taking the cat from him. 'Have you been exploring?'

'I found her,' Hal said, following Rada inside.

Despite its dark wooden furnishings, the huge room was light and airy because of two incredible arched picture windows that seemed to bring the Brocken into the room. He scanned the space, drawing the layout in his head, trying to take in as much detail as possible. This was the room where Clara had expected to stay: Alexander's room.

'She didn't climb up the tower, did she?' Freya asked.

'No.'

'She smelled delicious mouses, no doubt,' Rada said, rubbing her face in Belladonna's fur. The cat's amber eyes closed, and she started purring.

'She was trapped in the courtyard,' Hal said, noticing a strange array of items: small dark glass bottles, several funnels, a pestle and mortar, a perplexing-looking copper pot with a bowl at the bottom, a cylinder above it, and tubes protruding from the side, on a wooden desk that stood before one of the big windows. It looked like a medieval chemistry set.

'Belladonna goes wherever she wants,' Freya said, unpacking the suitcase, which lay open on a four-poster bed with red curtains. 'How do you like our tower? It was our playroom when we were children – Manfred, Alexander and I.'

'It's great,' Hal said as Freya took a portable hot plate from the case and brought it over to the desk. He pointed at the strange copper pot. 'What do you do with that?'

'Make potions,' Freya said happily, and clapped her hands together.

'This is where Freya works her magic,' Rada said proudly.

'Magic?' Hal approached the desk. Looking into a hessian bag, he saw it was filled with leaves that had a medicinal smell. He picked up a clear tub filled with moss and examined it.

Freya went to the window. 'Snow,' she muttered, watching the fat, fluffy flakes drift past. 'The white cloak that turns plants black and deadens the noise of man.' She turned to Rada. 'It is good that we brought our boots.'

'*Ja*,' Rada agreed, taking a pouch of cat food from a pocket on the side of Belladonna's basket and emptying it into a saucer on the floor.

While the women were distracted, Hal discreetly opened a drawer of Alexander Kratzenstein's desk a few centimetres. It was empty. He tried another, and another – all empty. What had he expected to find? A clue? The missing will? And then, with a jolt, he realized that there *was* a desk in which Alexander was much more likely to have kept important documents: the one on the train. 'I'd better go.'

'Thanks for bringing back Belladonna,' Freya said as he made his way to the door.

When Hal got into the lift, he pressed the button for the tower, then dropped to the carpeted floor and drew Freya's strange equipment. He was troubled by her joke about potions and Rada saying she made magic. What was that copper pot for? He couldn't imagine a use for the things on the desk, unless they *hadn't* been joking. Could the copper pot be a type of cauldron?

*

In the tower bedroom, Hilda, Ozan and Herman had their faces pressed to the window, talking excitedly to each other in German. The sky was a murky grey, an eiderdown of snow-laden cloud waiting to fall.

'The snow is heavy,' Ozan said to Hal. 'Tomorrow we can have a snowball fight and go sledging.'

Hal went into the turret to join them at the window and saw it was getting dark. He looked at his watch, a gift from his uncle last year when they'd gone travelling across America on the California Comet. It was after five o'clock. He looked out over Dead Man's Pass and felt a jolt.

A figure, a black silhouette, was walking away from the house along the railway tracks in the snow. Hal's breath misted the glass as he leaned closer. He wiped it with his sleeve, and glimpsed the figure disappeared into the cutting.

'Want to play video games?' Ozan asked him.

'In a bit,' Hal replied, staring at the space where the dark silhouette had disappeared. He went to his bed and dropped down, suddenly feeling deflated. He'd recognized the gait and shape of the figure in the snow. It was Uncle Nat out there, investigating on his own, just like he had last night in Berlin. Why hadn't he taken Hal with him?

'*Aaaarrrrghhhh!*' Hilda gave a blood-curdling scream that made Hal jump to his feet and spin round.

'*Fledermäuse! Fledermäuse!*' Ozan was yelling in German, waving his arms.

Herman was in his bunk, wailing like an air-raid siren.

Hal locked eyes with what was causing the commotion.

A large bat was frantically flapping
about the room in a panic,
bumping into the walls
and the furniture, diving
down, then swooping up.

Hilda was curled up in
a ball on her bed, staring
up at it through the gaps in
her fingers, screaming.

Herman hugged his knees to his
chest, calling out for his mama.

'Quick! Open all the windows,' Hal shouted, throwing
himself at the window closest to his bed and struggling with
the latch. Hilda sprang to her feet at her window, and Ozan
was in the other corner of the room. Herman seemed unable
to move.

As Hal got his window open, he heard something – a
distant laugh. A chill shot down his spine, but then he realized
to whom it belonged. Storming across the room, Hal bounded
up the stairs and yanked open the door to the upstairs room.

Arnie was on the floor with his arms hugged to his sides,
howling with laughter. In one of his hands he was clutching a
hessian sack. The room was dark but for the dingy light from
the little window and a red glow from the lantern embedded
in the model mountainside.

Hal grabbed Arnie and shook him, shouting, 'Help us, or
the bat will get hurt!'

Running back down the stairs, Hal pulled Herman to his

feet, standing him between Ozan and himself. 'Put your arms up and clap your hands together, making a noise.' Hal said, remembering that bats saw sonically. 'We'll try and drive it out of the window.'

Hilda ran, ducking with her hands over her head, to join their line, and a moment later Arnie was there too. The five of them made a wall of clapping, shouting humans, driving the bat towards the window beside Hilda's bed. The bat looped around the room once, then twice, before flying straight out of the window.

Ozan ran over and shut it, dropping down on to Hilda's bed with relief as they all turned to stare at Arnie.

'You should have seen your faces,' he crowed.

'That was cruel – to the bat,' Hal said angrily.

Arnie shrugged, unapologetic. 'Bats are always getting trapped in here. They hibernate in the tower roof.'

Hilda punched him as he walked past.

'Ouch!' Rubbing his arm and chuckling, Arnie pressed the button for the lift, and called out, 'You'd better make sure that door is closed properly, or when the colony wakes up hungry in the middle of the night, they might suck your blood.'

CHAPTER EIGHTEEN

DRAWING
AFTER DARK

Hal closed the windows and Ozan added a log to the fire and stoked it with a poker to warm up the room. Hilda took the throw from her bed and wrapped it round Herman like a cape, then double-checked that the door to the upper room was properly closed.

'Herman, have you read *Emil and the Detectives*?' Hilda asked, and Herman shook his head. 'It's really good. Would you like me to read a bit to you?'

Hal went and lay on his bed, listening to Hilda reading in German, and thought how impressive it was that she could speak so many languages. He slipped out his pocketbook and pen, turning to a clean page. He'd been trying not to admit it, but Uncle Nat had been acting weird ever since he'd met him at the school gates. His uncle was keeping something from him, something about his past, and it was an uncomfortable feeling. He wished he'd had the courage to ask him about HANGMAN. Why had Uncle Nat gone out to Dead

145

Man's Pass on his own? If he wanted to investigate, he could've come and found Hal. And where did he go last night in Berlin?

He leaned his pocketbook on his suitcase, drawing. His doodle turned into the corner of paper he'd seen sticking up out of Bertha's desk drawer. Was it the missing will?

It was too dark for him to venture out to Dead Man's Pass now, and he had no way of knowing where Uncle Nat had gone, so instead he made a list of the things he was going to investigate tomorrow morning:

1. Dead Man's Pass
2. Alexander's train carriage
3. Bertha's desk drawer
4. Uncle Nat

'What are you doing?' Hilda asked, approaching his bed and glancing down. 'Drawing?'

'No, nothing.' Hal snapped his pocketbook shut. 'I . . . er . . . it's private.'

'I understand.' Hilda perched on the end of the bed. 'I keep a diary too. What were you writing about?'

'This creepy old house,' Hal replied.

'Isn't it magnificent?' Hilda said, her eyes shining. 'It's full of stories. I love it.'

'Tomorrow, I propose we have snowball war!' Ozan declared from across the room. 'We'll divide into two teams, make snowballs, and then –' he brought his hands together with a clap – 'fight it out.'

'Let's do it in Dead Man's Pass,' Hal suggested, thinking the snow would give him the perfect cover for a spot of investigating. 'If we see any witches, we can take them down.' He mimed throwing a snowball at an imaginary witch, and Herman giggled.

'I want to build a snowman,' he said.

'Ooh, me too!' Hilda agreed. 'We can get a carrot for his nose from the kitchen and coal from the bucket by the fire in the salon for buttons and eyes.'

Excited chatter about tomorrow's snow day swept aside all thoughts of the library and Arnie's bat attack, and spirits rose as Herman told them that he was certain there were two sledges out in the train shed.

'I'd love to get a look at the old tank engine,' Hal said, thinking he might be able to sneak into Alexander's train carriage if he was left alone in the shed for long enough.

'Boy, you *do* like trains,' Ozan said.

'Trains are awesome,' Hal replied.

It was dark, and the moon a hazy circle of light behind the clouds, when Alma arrived with a silver trolley laden with food.

'Dinner is served!' she announced, wheeling the trolley into the room.

'Aren't we eating downstairs?' Hal asked.

'No, the grown-ups will ruin your food with their sour faces and dull conversations,' Alma said cheerfully. 'I thought it would be much more fun for you to eat dinner up here by the fire, without having to listen to our boring talk about the funeral.'

Herman was smiling and nodding, and Hal could see that Hilda and Ozan were happy with this arrangement too, but his heart sank. He'd been hoping to talk to his uncle at dinner. They'd not had a moment alone together all day. He had questions he wanted answered.

Herman took the cutlery from the trolley, while Hilda put the pillows from their beds on the rug for them to sit on. Dinner was *Käsespätzle*, which it turned out was the German equivalent of macaroni cheese, with mini dumplings instead of macaroni. It was tasty, and Hal polished off the lot.

Alma sat on the edge of Hilda's bed, happily plaiting her granddaughter's hair while they ate. 'What have you children been up to this afternoon?'

Ozan told her about Arnie's mean trick with the bat, and she was scandalized on the the bat's behalf, then Herman told her about Hal getting frightened by Adalwolf, and they all laughed.

'Oma, what do you know about Frau Babelin?' Hilda asked, and they fell silent, waiting for her response.

'I know that her name is used to scare children into behaving well. I know that she was the woman who cursed the Kratzensteins for the death of her son . . .' She paused.

'Do you believe in her?' Ozan pressed.

Alma thought for a moment, and then said, 'Ever since I was a girl and first visited this house, I have heard stories of a woman who lives in the woods on the mountain. Those who've seen her always describe her the same way: as having a grey, hooded cloak spun from the Brocken mists, a ghostly

pale complexion, long black hair, and eyes as dark as tunnels into the underworld. Once, when I was sixteen and we were visiting Arnold, I decided to go for a walk up the mountain on my own. In the forest, I glimpsed a woman with dark eyes, who turned my skin to gooseflesh and then disappeared.' She shook her head. 'I don't know if it was Frau Babelin – the woman in the woods – or someone just taking a walk, but she turned my blood to ice. I ran all the way back to my mother.' She shrugged.

Hal was struck by how similar Alma's depiction of the witch was to Connie's description of her encounter with the woman in the forest, and yet there must have been forty years between the two episodes.

'Knock, knock,' came a sweet voice, and they turned to see Connie entering with an overloaded tray. She was concentrating so hard on not spilling the five hot chocolates she was balancing on the tray that her tongue was sticking out. 'I come with ice cream, hot chocolate and hot-water bottles.'

They all cheered, and she beamed as she set down the tray on Hilda's bed. Pulling a hot-water bottle from the cloth bag slung across her chest, she put it in Hal's bed, then took one out for Herman's, another for Ozan's and finally Hilda's. 'It's going to be a cold night,' she said.

'How are they getting on downstairs?' Alma asked with meaning.

'They're about to serve dinner,' Connie replied. 'You should go down and eat. I've already eaten. Dinner is family only.' She picked up two bowls of ice cream. 'Who wants ice cream?' she asked, and rewarded Ozan and Herman's loud cries of 'Me!' with a bowl each, as Alma said goodbye and went downstairs.

'It isn't very friendly of them not to invite you to dinner,' Herman said to Connie.

'It's fine,' Connie replied, putting the tray of drinks on the floor in the middle of them, picking up a mug and sitting down cross-legged. 'I'll bet you're having a lot more fun up here than they are down there.'

150

'Are Mama and Bertha still cross with each other?' Herman asked.

'I don't really know what it's about,' Connie replied, not answering the question.

'Papa's money,' Herman said matter-of-factly. 'He had a lot of money and owned most of K-Bahn. Mama is worried Bertha will take all of it, and because she is Opa's favourite and he loves Arnie better than me we will have to leave our home in Berlin.'

'Herman, that's not true, is it?' Hilda gasped.

'I don't care.' Herman shrugged as he spooned ice cream into his mouth. 'I don't want to own K-Bahn. I want to be a pianist.'

'I'm sure Arnold wouldn't let Bertha do anything to upset you or your mother,' Connie reassured him. 'And he's very strict about not having favourite grandchildren. He has told me how beautifully you play the piano. He's very proud of you.'

Herman blushed with pleasure.

Hal thought about Alexander's will. If he had been murdered, the contents of the will could provide a motive. If Herman was right, and the will concerned the shares he owned in K-Bahn, then perhaps he needed to look for someone interested in taking over the rail company. Immediately his mind jumped to Arnie, but surely he wouldn't want any harm to come to his own father.

'So, what are you children planning to do tomorrow?' Connie asked, changing the subject. 'The snow looks nice and deep.'

'We're going to have a snowball war in Dead Man's Pass,'

Ozan declared, and Connie laughed at his excitement.

'That sounds fun.'

'I'm going to build a giant snowman,' Herman told her.

'I want to see the old tank engine,' Hal said. 'Do you think Aksel will show it to me?'

'Aksel would enjoy showing the engine to you. He loves that machine.'

'Are Aksel and Arnie good friends?' Hal asked, surprising her with his question.

'Yes, although Aksel is more like a big brother to Arnie than a friend.'

'I bet Aksel doesn't believe in Frau Babelin,' Ozan said.

'No? Then why does he wear a locket round his neck to ward off her evil?'

'A locket?' Hilda was thrilled. 'Does he?'

'You look tomorrow, if you don't believe me,' Connie said, sipping her drink. 'He never takes it off.'

There was a silence as they all thought about a man as big and strong and gruff as Aksel fearing the witch.

'I wish I could go back to Berlin,' Herman said quietly. 'I don't like the Brocken.'

'You don't think you'll live in this house one day?' Connie asked.

Herman looked horrified. 'No! I hate it. Mama hates it, even Papa didn't like to come back here.'

'Thousands of tourists come to the Brocken every year,' Connie said. 'It's considered to be a place of great natural beauty.'

'Yes, but then they go home again, to their nice safe

houses,' Herman said, and she laughed.

'Good point.' She looked around at the children. 'It's nice having people in the house to talk to.'

Connie suggested a game of charades, but Hal didn't know any of the German books or TV programmes they acted out, so they decided only to do big American movies, giving him a chance of joining in.

Alma returned, telling them it was time for bed, and they each took it in turns to clean their teeth in the little bathroom under the stairs.

Hal found a torch in the drawers beside his bed, and later that night, after they had turned the lights out and he could hear the others breathing heavily, he wriggled down under his duvet and switched it on.

As the wind howled around the tower, hurling snow at its windows, Hal knelt in the hot-water-bottle warmth of his duvet tent, took out his pocketbook and pen, and drew all the images crowding his head: Arnie hiding up in the tower with the bats; Uncle Nat walking alone in the snow; Arnold looking out of the window at Dead Man's Pass; Freya clutching her strange cauldron, Belladonna at her feet; and Aksel with a necklace round his neck to ward off evil. Tomorrow he was determined to get answers to every single one of his questions.

CHAPTER NINETEEN

STINKING GOAT

Hal woke up, blinking as his eyes adjusted to the dazzling glow of snow light streaming in the turret windows.

'You are bright awake?' Ozan whispered from his bunk, and Hal saw he was already dressed, sitting cross-legged.

'It's *wide* awake,' Hal replied sleepily, 'and no, I'm not.'

'Come on, don't you want to get out there, in the snow?'

Hal sat up. He *did* want to get out there, into Dead Man's Pass, and investigate. 'Give me a minute.' He threw his legs out of bed and pulled on thick socks. Two minutes later, he was dressed in his warmest clothes.

Ozan clambered down the ladder, whispering, 'Shall I wake the others?'

Hal shook his head. 'Let's go to the train shed first – see if we can find those sledges?'

Ozan eyed him suspiciously. 'You want to see the steam engine.'

'Well, yeah, but, also . . .' He lowered his voice to a

whisper. 'Yesterday, when Hilda was investigating the curse, and Herman told us about his dad looking terrified, it got me wondering. What could have frightened him so badly that he died?'

'Do you think it was the witch? Frau Babelin?'

'We could do a bit of investigating now, before Herman wakes up. There might be a clue in Alexander Kratzenstein's train carriage. That's in the train shed too.'

Ozan's eyes lit up. He glanced at his sleeping sister. 'If we find a clue, Hilda will be so jealous.'

'And we'd be helping Herman.'

'Let's do it.'

The boys snuck out of the house, the snow crunching under their feet as they followed the half-buried rails out of the cobbled courtyard. Hal hoped they were early enough that no one would be about.

A noise, like a baby crying out, startled him, and he grabbed Ozan's arm, stopping dead. 'What was that?'

Ozan chuckled and pointed through the lofty fir trees beyond the train shed. Behind a wire fence stood two skinny-legged goats, one white with a beard and horns, the other rust red with pale splotches.

'Goats! Why does old Arnold keep goats?' Hal exclaimed, hoping Ozan wouldn't notice his blushing. A line from Uncle Nat's book *Faust* came into his head – *Over stream and fern, gorse and ditch, Tramp stinking goat and farting witch* – but these goats seemed quite cute.

The big doors to the train shed were open. It was gloomy

inside, and the air was thick with the heavenly smell of diesel oil and coal dust.

'Wow,' whispered Ozan as they clapped eyes on the vintage black tank engine with blood-red buffer beam and pistons. It was polished up as if it were new. A tall chimney sprouted up from the circular boiler face, which was framed by a triangle of three lanterns.

The shed was wide enough to accommodate the two engines and several carriages. The blue Bombardier TRAXX was on a wider set of rails a couple of metres from the Class 99.

'Hello?' Hal called out, to see if they were alone, but there was a clatter of tools and Aksel emerged from the shadows in grease-stained overalls. He greeted the boys with a grunt as he picked up a rag to wipe his hands.

Hal pointed at the tank engine. 'Beautiful.'

Aksel nodded and patted the loco.

'Can we look?' Hal said, pointing to try and communicate. 'Go on the footplate?'

Aksel nodded, and stepped back to allow Hal and Ozan to climb up.

Eagerly Hal grabbed the rail and pulled himself into the cab. Ozan was a step behind him. The brass pipes shone; there wasn't a mark on them. A fire had been laid in the boiler, but not lit. He realized Aksel was getting the loco ready for the funeral tomorrow.

'This is the regulator,' Hal said to Ozan, pointing to the lever. 'That's the steam chest pressure gauge.' He pointed at the dial in front of him. 'Main boiler pressure gauge.' He pointed to another dial, then touched a red wheel. 'Injector steam valve.' He put his finger to a switch in a pipe. 'And this, I think, is the whistle.'

'Good.' Aksel nodded, looking impressed.

'You can drive a steam train?' Ozan was astonished.

'Well, no, it takes years of training, but I know how they work.' Hal dropped his voice to a whisper. 'How are we going to get into the carriage without Aksel seeing?'

'I'll ask him to show me where the sledges are,' Ozan replied.

'Good idea.'

Ozan jumped down from the footplate, speaking to Aksel in German. Hal looked down and saw that hanging over the collar of Aksel's T-shirt was a gold locket. He shifted to get a clearer view. The oval of gold was the size of his thumb, with an ornate floral engraving, in the centre of which was a pair of initials that sent a chill down Hal's spine.

Aksel pointed to the back of the train shed, sending Ozan to get the sledges on his own. Ozan shot Hal an apologetic look.

'Aksel?' Hal clambered down the ladder. 'Do you understand English?'

'Little,' Aksel raised his hand, pinching his thumb and forefinger close.

'Were you here when Alexander Kratzenstein died?'

The muscles around Aksel's eyes tightened at the question, but he gave a curt nod.

'Who found him?'

'Bertha.' Aksel's eyes lost their focus as he remembered. 'She scream and scream.'

'What did you do?' Hal whispered.

'I run. I find her in the dark.' He patted his chest. 'I carry Alexander home.'

'His face . . .' But Hal didn't need to finish. Aksel's eyes grew dark, and his nostrils flared as he shook his head, and Hal knew he'd seen the expression of horror. 'What do you think happened?'

'Frau Babelin,' Aksel growled, his hand going to his locket as he turned his head towards the house. 'They must pay.'

'*Aksel? Wo bist du?*' Connie called into the shed.

Aksel hurriedly stuffed his rag into a pocket and ran a hand through his hair. '*Hier,*' he called out, walking into the light of the open door.

'*Eine der Ziegen fehlt. Es gibt ein Loch im Zaun. Ich denke sie ist entkommen!*'

'Hello,' Hal came to Aksel's side.

'Good morning, Harrison.' Connie smiled. 'What are you doing here?' Hal looked at the tank engine and Connie laughed. 'Of course! I'm sorry I must take Aksel away. There's nothing he likes better than talking about how that machine

158

works, but one of Arnold's goats has escaped. I need Aksel to help me find it and get it back in the pen.' She stared at Hal for a second, then said, 'You are not wearing your glasses today?'

Hal felt like she'd just thrown a bucket of icy water over him. He'd left his glasses beside his bed. He'd been so keen to investigate that he'd forgotten about his disguise. 'I don't want to break them. I'm long-sighted, I only need them for close-up stuff. We're having a snowball fight, then going sledging.'

As if by magic, Ozan came forward dragging a pair of red plastic sledges, and Connie laughed. She linked her arm through Aksel's, and the pair of them walked away in the direction of the goat pen.

'Quick,' Hal whispered.

Ozan let go of the sledge ropes and hurried after Hal, who'd run to the carriage they'd travelled in from Berlin.

'Did you see the locket round Aksel's neck?' Hal whispered. 'It has two initials engraved on it – a *G* and a *B*.' He looked at Ozan, waiting for him to make the connection.

'Gobel Babelin?'

'Why would he have a locket with her initials on? Do you think Aksel could be related to her?'

The boys exchanged an alarmed look.

'Let's be quick, before he gets back,' Hal said, trying the door to the carriage. It opened with a squeak. The two boys stepped inside and looked around. 'We mustn't move anything, or, if we do, we must make sure we put it back exactly where we found it.'

They each took a side of the carriage and made a thorough

159

sweep of each shelf and surface, meeting at the desk below Alexander's portrait.

'What are we looking for?' Ozan asked.

'Alexander Kratzenstein's will,' Hal said.

Ozan stiffened. 'His will? But won't Clara have that already?'

'It's missing – that's why the adults are all shouting at each other,' Hal replied, cursing himself for letting that bit of information slip out. Remembering that he was meant to be long-sighted, he lifted out a plastic folder of letters from the top desk drawer and clumsily dropped it to the floor scattering the pages. 'Drat! I wish I'd brought my glasses.' He waved at the letters on the floor. 'I can't read these.'

'You couldn't anyway. It's all in German.' Ozan gathered the pages together and began to look through them.

'Does any of it look like a will?'

'No, it's all letters between Alexander and some company,' said Ozan. 'I'll keep looking.' He passed the wodge of pages to Hal, who returned them to their plastic folder. At the top of the papers Hal noticed the logo of the firm that was corresponding with Alexander Kratzenstein was a zigzag of three mountain peaks above the word *Stromacre*.

'There's nothing here.' Ozan checked the last drawer. 'We should go before Aksel comes back.'

There was one other place that Hal thought Alexander's missing will could be, but he didn't relish the idea of going back into Bertha's room.

CHAPTER TWENTY

DEAD MAN'S PASS

The two boys, each dragging a sledge, marched out of the train shed on to the untrodden snow.

'There's Hilda and Herman!' Ozan nodded towards the courtyard entrance, and Hal saw the pair rolling a snowball the size of a pumpkin. 'They're making a snowman.'

'Where did you disappear to?' Hilda called out, waving.

Ozan pointed to the sledges by way of reply. 'Wait till Hilda hears what you saw on Aksel's locket,' he said. 'She'll freak out.'

'Don't say anything in front of Herman. We don't want to frighten him.'

'We came out to find you,' Hilda said, looking from Ozan to Hal, obviously unhappy about being left behind. 'Why did you sneak off without us?'

'Hal wanted to look at the steam engine,' Ozan said, and Hal nodded. 'And I found the sledges. We were just coming to get you.'

'If we go to the other end of Dead Man's Pass, it's downhill all way back to the house,' Herman said. 'It's really fun to sledge down the rail tracks.'

Excited by this idea, they set off towards the pass. Ozan pulled on his gloves and scooped up some snow, packing it solid in his fist and then firing it at Hal, who jumped back just in time.

'Missed me,' Hal crowed as Hilda aimed a snowball at the back of Ozan's head, scoring a direct hit.

Hal threw a snowball at Herman, missing on purpose. Herman's retaliatory snowballs were small, but he was a good shot. He fired a barrage of snowballs at Hal and the three powder bombs exploded one after another on Hal's chest, shoulder and upper arm. The four of them chased each other, laughing and dodging, firing and feigning, along the railway tracks, but their laughter died away when they reached the mouth of Dead Man's Pass.

'I see the skull,' Ozan said. 'There, in the wall of the pass. That overhanging rock is the forehead and below it, see those holes?' The gaping cavities that made the top of the face were devoid of snow. 'They are the eyes. That triangle gap between them is the nose.'

'There's no mouth,' Hal said. He looked at Herman. 'Is that it? Is that the skull face Arnie was talking about? It's not very spooky.'

Herman nodded. 'Opa puts pumpkin lanterns in the eyeholes at Halloween. It looks spooky then.'

The rails curved into the pass, and Hal was surprised by how narrow it was – no wider than a farm track. The towering

162

rock walls made the cutting feel claustrophobic, and once they were inside, the acoustics amplified that feeling. Any noise in the pass echoed off the walls, but all sounds from the outside world were silenced.

Hal had to admit that, from inside the pass, the skull was scarier. The eyes glared down at him, unblinking, and the lack of a jawbone gave the impression that it had opened its mouth wide, as if to swallow them up. He recalled Arnie's story of encountering the witch here and him saying the eyes were glowing. He could see how that would be terrifying. He looked around, wondering where Alexander's body had been found, but the snow had covered up all possible clues, including Uncle Nat's tracks from last night. Was that why his uncle had come out here? Did he want to check for clues before the snow fell? Hal realized that would have been a good idea.

'The mist looks like the Brocken's breath,' Hilda said, looking up at the flattened peak of the mountain and the icy vapour lacing through the treetops. 'We won't have a blue sky for long.'

'I changed my mind.' Herman shivered, 'I don't want to go sledging. I want to go back and finish the snowman.'

'Don't be afraid,' Ozan said, linking arms with Herman. 'We'll take care of you.'

Herman laughed nervously. 'I'm not afraid.'

Hilda took Herman's free hand and gave him a comforting smile. 'If you're worried, we can go back . . .'

'I'm not scared,' Herman insisted, looking terrified. He

163

shook them off and grabbed the ropes of Ozan's sledge, marching through the pass, dragging it behind him.

Hal hurried to fall in step beside him. 'How about we go on the sledge together? It'll go much faster. We may be able to ride it all the way back to the house.'

Herman nodded, but didn't reply.

The pass was the length of three lorries, end to end. When they came out the other side, Hal saw that the railway track merged with another, which climbed the Brocken. A dark forest of gigantic fir trees lined the slopes either side of it.

The four children set up their two sledges on the narrow rails of the track.

'We'll go first,' Ozan said, as Hilda clambered on to the front of their sledge, taking the steering ropes in her hands. Resting his hands on her shoulders, Ozan ran forward fast, pushing the sledge off, then dropped to his knees behind his sister. They rocketed down the pass, whooping and yelling, their jubilant shouts bouncing off the rock walls.

Herman laughed as Hilda and Ozan shot out of the pass at the other end, both coming off the sledge and landing in a heap in the snow. He looked at Hal. 'Start slower. We'll pick up speed, but not so much that we'll fall off the rails.'

Herman sat at the front with his knees up against his chest, holding on to the steering rope. Hal sat down with his legs out straight, either side of Herman.

'You ready?' Hal asked, reaching behind him and grabbing a rail with each hand. Herman nodded and Hal pushed off.

They slid slowly at first and Hal leaned forward, helping the sledge pick up speed. He glimpsed something move above them and looked up. At the top of the pass, his eye caught the whirling of grey cloth, then he heard the scattershot of falling stones. '*Let go of the ropes!*' he shouted, flinging his arms round Herman and launching them both off the sledge. As they landed in the snow, Hal tightened his grip round the boy and rolled, so that Herman was sandwiched safely between the rock wall and Hal.

With a thunderous clatter, a landslide of stones and snow smashed down on to their empty sledge.

CHAPTER TWENTY-ONE

WITCH'S PRINTS

'*Bist du in Ordnung?*' Hilda cried as she and Ozan ran to the entrance of the cutting.

Hal looked up cautiously, fearful of more missiles from above, but Dead Man's Pass was silent. He patted Herman. 'We're OK. Come on.' He got to his feet and helped Herman up, who was staring with horror at the battered sledge.

'We could have died,' he whispered, his breath coming in wheezes.

'No,' Hal replied dismissively, trying to hide how shaken he felt. 'We might have got a bump on the head and had a few scratches, but that's all. Come on, let's get out of here.' He grabbed the sledge ropes and Herman's hand, then hurried towards Hilda and Ozan.

'You saved my life.' Herman looked at him with wide eyes. 'Thank you.'

'What are cousins for?' Hal replied with a warm smile.

'Are you OK?' Hilda asked.

'What happened?' Ozan asked.

'I think the snow, and your whooping, dislodged some loose stones,' Hal lied. 'I heard them falling, and rolled us to safety.' He pulled the sledge forward so they could see the dented and slashed plastic. 'Good job, really.'

'Oh!' Hilda gasped, then seeing that Herman was shivering she put her arm round him. 'That must've been a terrible shock, Herman. Are you all right? You know what we all need? Some breakfast. Come on, let's go back to the house. I'm starving.'

'There are stones on the track,' Hal said, not moving. 'We should clear them. It's dangerous to leave them there.'

'I'll help you,' Ozan said.

'We'll meet you back at the house,' Hal said, and Hilda nodded, walking Herman away from Dead Man's Pass.

'Quick, come with me,' Hal said, hurrying back along the track, looking up. When they reached the rockfall, Ozan bent and started clearing them off the tracks, but Hal tugged his arm. 'We need to find a way up,' he whispered. 'Someone was up there just before the stones fell.'

Running through the pass, studying the walls, Hal saw there was no way up. At the other end, where they had set their sledges, he spotted goat footprints in the snow, and a track up the incline that wove between fir trees. 'This way,' he called, not waiting for Ozan as he climbed higher, slipping and sliding on the snow, using the trees to propel himself along. The shock of what had happened in the pass was only now sinking in and he was angry. Had someone sent down that shower of stones on purpose?

By the time they reached the crest of the cutting, Hal knew

whoever he'd seen up here was long gone.

'We're too late,' he said as Ozan scrambled up beside him.

'You said it was our shouts and the snow that caused the stones to fall,' Ozan said, leaning against a tree trunk as he paused to catch his breath.

'I said that so Herman wouldn't be frightened. I saw someone.'

'What did you see?'

'A grey cloak.'

'No face?'

Hal shook his head.

'Do you think it was the witch?'

'Or someone looking like the witch,' Hal said, climbing on to a boulder. He turned slowly, scanning the landscape, taking in every detail of what he saw around him, first in the foreground at his feet, and then expanding his view, taking in details further away, right up to the horizon. He looked for shadows among the tree trunks, movement beyond the pass. The snow helped. He saw his and Ozan's footprints, and then a set of larger prints in the snow.

'What are you doing?' Ozan asked, climbing up beside him.

'Looking.' Hal pointed to the set of large footprints. 'I was right. There was someone up here. You can see deep footprints where they kicked those stones free.' He jumped down, placing his own foot beside one of the larger prints, then removed it. 'I'm a size six. This print is much bigger, and look – it has a round toe. It looks like a man's boot.'

'If we had a camera, we could take a picture.'

'I've got a notebook.' Hal pulled it from his pocket with his pen. 'I could try and draw it?'

'Um, okay,' Ozan said, not looking convinced.

'You keep a lookout.' Hal didn't want Ozan to watch him draw. He needed to make his picture appear basic, but wanted to get the difference in scale of the two footprints, and the tread on the perpetrator's boot, right.

Ozan nodded, and scanned the horizon from the rock, like Hal had.

Hal quickly sketched his own footprint and then, beside it, the larger boot print. He guessed the boot print was a size ten — definitely a man's shoe. He drew the chunky pattern on the sole, noticing it was worn down on the inner heel.

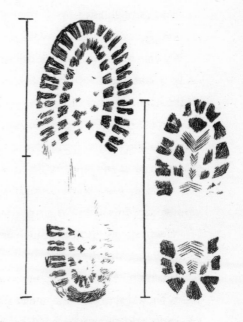

'Hal . . . someone is moving down there.' Ozan pointed in the direction the footprints led.

'Let's see if we can catch up with them,' Hal said, putting his pocketbook away, as Ozan jumped down.

The pair half ran, half slid down the rocky hillside, trying to stay low and catch up to their quarry.

'Stop,' Ozan whispered, grabbing the back of Hal's anorak and pulling him to the ground. He put his finger to his lips, then pointed.

Peering through the snow-covered undergrowth, Hal saw a figure in a black hooded cloak, three or four metres away, squatting down beside a fallen tree, studying its mossy, ivy-clad roots. His heartbeat pulsed in his ears. He saw a pair of hiking boots poking out from the bottom of the cloak. As the figure straightened up, it drew a wooden-handled knife, gripping it in their right hand.

Hal held his breath, squashing himself down into the snow.

A sound of snapping sticks and footsteps caused the cloaked figure to turn, and the hood fell back.

'Freya!' Ozan whispered in horror.

Rada came over to her, carrying a basket stuffed with bark, evergreen twigs and pine needles. Sitting in the basket, playing with a twig, was Belladonna. The two women exchanged whispered words. Freya cut something from the fallen tree. Straightening up, Freya added whatever it was she'd removed from the tree into the basket, stroking the cat before slipping her arm through Rada's. The boys watched them walk away.

'What did they say?' Hal asked Ozan.

'Freya said the snow made harvesting difficult and they should have done this last time they were here.'

'But Freya told us she hasn't been back to Schloss Kratzenstein for years.'

Ozan shrugged. 'Then she said they must go to the stream, to get water.'

Hal was baffled as to what any of this could mean.

'Do you think Freya kicked those stones down on Dead Man's Pass? Is she the witch?' asked Ozan.

'I don't know.' Hal thought of the strange copper pot in her room.

'What should we do?'

'Can you follow Freya and Rada, from a distance, and listen to what they're saying?' Hal asked. 'I want to go back to the pass and check something.'

'*Ja.*' Ozan jumped up, excited by idea of tailing Freya and Rada. 'Meet you in the *Kinderturm.*'

CHAPTER TWENTY-TWO

RATTED OUT

Hal waited till Ozan was out of sight before he pulled his pocketbook out. Flipping to a clean page, he drew the crouched, hooded form of Freya, her boots peeping out from her cloak, her knife in her hand. She had lied when she'd said she'd not been home for years. Why? When was she last here? Was it the weekend Alexander had died? Holding his sketch at arm's length he realized it looked as if he'd drawn a witch. He inspected the fallen tree to see what she had been sawing at with her knife and found a sheared-off nub with some traces of tree sap. He placed his foot beside her footprints in the snow. Freya's feet were the same size as his. It couldn't have been her that he'd seen looking down on Dead Man's Pass.

Making his way round to the far entrance of Dead Man's Pass, Hal returned to the spot where he'd looked up to see the whirling grey cloak. He scoured the full length of the cutting, hunting for any clue that might shed light on who'd created the rockfall. All he found was a new set of man-sized footprints through the cutting.

'Hey, Skull Face,' Hal said to the vacant stone eyes looking down at him. 'Did you see what happened the night Alexander died? If only you had a jaw, you could tell me.' Then he had an idea. Grabbing an edge of rock, Hal put his foot into a niche, and climbed up until he could see into the gaping eyeholes.

Reaching into the left eye socket, Hal pulled out the charred circular stump of a big candle. There was one in the

right eye socket too. Thinking back to what Herman had said, he wondered if they were left there from Halloween, or were they new? Brushing the snow off the ridge of rock that made the nose, he worked his fingers into the cracks, and reached into the two joined holes that made the skull's nostrils. His fist touched something soft and he snatched his hand back with a gasp.

Peering into the dark cavity, he saw nothing. Steeling himself, he pulled on his glove and shoved his hand back into the hole, swiftly yanking out whatever it was inside, overbalancing and jumping down to the ground.

In his hand was a small silky black bag. He loosened the drawstring and pulled out two circular discs, one of white face paint, one of black. Staring at the pancakes of paint, his skin prickled. He felt certain this was a clue relating to Alexander's death. He returned the make-up to its hiding place and jumped down to the ground, pulling out his pocketbook. He drew the skull face, marking where he'd found the candle stubs and the make-up. Then went and cleared the stones away from the railway tracks. The funeral train would be travelling through the pass tomorrow morning and he didn't want there to be an accident.

Hearing a high mournful whistle, Hal felt a dart of joy and ran to the end of the pass, where he could see the Brockenbahn line. The chuffing of the approaching steam engine, and oyster-grey plume of smoke from the chimney, came before the imposing black-and-red glossy face of the locomotive he'd seen in Wernigerode the previous day.

Running parallel with the track, Hal raced the train up the Brocken until he ran out of puff and had to stop. The train rattled past him, and the driver tooted the whistle as Hal waved.

Up ahead, the train slowed, and Hal saw that beyond the point where the Kratzenstein spur met the main line there was a low wooden platform with a bench and a shelter. It was a station, and sitting on the bench was a man Hal recognized. It was Uncle Nat.

Instinctively, Hal stepped back from the tracks, hiding in the shadow of the trees. He approached stealthily. What was Uncle Nat doing at the station? Was he going to catch the train?

The train stopped. Carriage doors clicked open and slammed shut. A handful of hikers alighted, but Uncle Nat remained on the bench.

The train left, huffing gouts of smoke into the misty air as it continued its climb up the Brocken.

Uncle Nat got up, walking along the platform to a noticeboard, which he appeared to read as the hikers disappeared along the trail into the woods. Then he went to the very end and stooped to tie his shoelace. He straightened up, checked his watch, stepped down from the platform, and Hal watched him walk along the rails back towards Schloss Kratzenstein.

Waiting until he was certain his uncle had gone, Hal crossed the hiking trail on to the small station. He sat on the

bench where Uncle Nat had sat, looking all around it, then peered up and down the tracks. He went to the noticeboard. Everything was in German except one English announcement about a change of timetable in the tourist season. Hal went to the end of the platform beside the low wooden fence, where his uncle had tied his shoelace, and crouched down beside frozen leaf mulch and snow. He slipped his fingers under the icy disc of rotten leaves, lifting it up. He cried out, letting it drop. Beneath it was a dead rat with milky white eyes.

Hal looked about, trying to ignore the rat's grey tail, which was sticking out. Why would Uncle Nat walk to this station, watch a train pass, read a German noticeboard, tie his shoelace next to a dead rat, and then go back to the house? He was missing something. He looked at the grey tail. Was the rat here to put people off looking? Pulling on his gloves, he lifted the leaf mulch again, picking the rat up by its tail. Keeping it at arm's length, he poked about in the snow, but there was nothing there.

The rat dangling from his thumb and forefinger was surprisingly light. Peering at it, he noticed a thin line, as if made by a scalpel blade, under the rat's neck.

'When is a rat not a rat?' he whispered, putting it on the ground and pulling at the line. It came apart, and Hal saw it was kept closed by a thin strip of Velcro. His heart skipped. Inside, where the rodent should have had a stomach, there was a small scroll of paper. Hal looked over his shoulder, scanning the trees. Had Uncle Nat put the paper in the rat? He took it out and unravelled it. Written on it was a message in pencil that made no sense. It was a sequence of letters and numbers. It was in code.

Pulling out his pocketbook, Hal copied down the code. He shoved the book back in his pocket and returned the note to the cavity inside the rat as quickly he could. His hands were shaking. He knew he was doing something that he shouldn't, that he'd discovered something Uncle Nat didn't want him to know about. He sealed the rat and slid it back under the frozen leaf mulch. Getting up, he tried to look nonchalant as he sauntered back down the platform and dropped down on to the tracks. Out out of the corner of his eye, in the shadow of the trees, he thought he glimpsed a woman with dark eyes watching him. He was unable to stop himself from breaking into a run.

CHAPTER TWENTY-THREE

BEAR FRUIT

Hal ran up the steps to the front door of Schloss Kratzenstein. It wasn't locked. Once inside the grand entrance hall, he stopped to catch his breath. He heard a series of high musical notes, and the hairs on the back of his neck rose. He scolded himself for having the heebie-jeebies. The music was someone playing the piano, probably Herman. He told himself that no one had been watching him back at the station. He'd imagined it. His eyes came to rest on a door under the stairs, and he remembered Herman saying it was a bathroom. He needed somewhere private to sort through the maelstrom of thoughts thundering around his head.

Pushing open the door, Hal gave a strangled squeal of fright and his knees buckled as he stared up into the black eyes of an eight-foot bear, standing on its back legs, baring its teeth, its paws raised and claws out. Slumping against the wall, his hand over his hammering heart, Hal inwardly cursed old Arnold for his taxidermy tricks. He locked the door, pulled out his pocketbook, put down the lid of the toilet and sat staring at the note that he'd hurriedly copied down.

$3956\text{-}7.$ $N_2OI_2I_2UKO$ $WOBONHOR.$ $EUTKN_2UT$
$ROUBT_2NHUT_2OR.$ NC AC_2W $RWNOR\text{-}C_2I$
$VI_2I_2OT_2$ $NI_2T'T_2$ $BAN_2IWAN_2NI_2OR,$ N $E_2NU_2U_2$
I_2T_2UTR $RAE_2T.$ T_2EO BUI_2O NI_2 ONT_2EOW
$TUT_2C_2WUU_2$ AW U $RAN_2OI_2T_2NB$ $BWNN_2O.$
T_2EO $XNKTUU_2N_2UT$

It had been written by his uncle – Hal recognized the handwriting. But what did it mean? He hoped, by looking at the letters and numbers, that he might see a pattern or glean some crumb of understanding from them, but ten minutes passed and he was still clueless. Who was Uncle Nat leaving coded messages for? Was he somehow mixed up in what had happened to Alexander Kratzenstein? Was this something to do with the baron and HANGMAN?

'I need Hilda,' Hal muttered. 'She'll know how to read this.'

Getting to his feet, he went to the sink and splashed cold water on his face. He needed to calm down and focus. He knew that things were often most confusing immediately before a truthful picture started forming in his head. He realized he was hungry. He hadn't had breakfast. No one could think properly with an empty stomach.

He made his way through the covered courtyard and the salon to the kitchen. A selection of breakfast meats, cheeses and bread had been left on the table, along with a stack of glasses and a jug of orange juice. He grabbed a roll, filling it with salami and cheese. As he ate, he went to the back door, curious about what was on the other side. He found a walled kitchen garden that led to the impressive greenhouse. He saw a gate in the brick wall and crossed the unblemished snow to open it. It led to the railway platform. On the tracks he saw a lone black carriage. The door handles were polished silver, the windows were dressed with black lace curtains, and Hal understood immediately that this was the Kratzenstein funeral carriage. From inside, he could hear the high, gentle sobs of a woman, and knew he shouldn't be listening to this intensely personal expression of grief. Feeling like a trespasser, Hal crept back through the gate, closing it silently, and returned to the kitchen, picking up more food from the table before making his way to the tower.

Hilda was on her own, reading.

'Where's Herman? Is he OK?' Hal asked.

'He went to play the piano. He said it calms him down. He's frightened, because of the accident with the sledge, but he doesn't want us to tell the grown-ups. He doesn't want to make a fuss before the funeral or to worry his mum.'

Hal wondered if it was Clara he'd heard crying in the funeral carriage.

'You're his hero.' Hilda grinned.

'Harrison!' Ozan burst through the door, breathless, carrying a boot and a shoe. 'You'll never guess what I have discovered.'

'What's going on?' Hilda asked, looking from Ozan to Hal.

'We've been detectives,' Ozan replied.

Hilda crossed her arms angrily. 'You said being a detective was boring! It was my idea to investigate the curse. This is *my* case.'

'We can't help it if we keep discovering clues.' Ozan laughed at Hilda's scowl.

Hal could see they were about to argue. 'Hilda, when Ozan and I went to the train shed this morning to get the sledges, we saw Aksel's locket, the one Connie told us about.'

'It has the initials *GB* on it,' Ozan blurted out.

The frown lines disappeared from Hilda's forehead as her eyebrows lifted. 'Gobel Babelin?'

Ozan nodded. 'We think Aksel could be related to the witch!'

'I asked him what he thought had happened to Alexander,' Hal told her. 'He said the Kratzensteins *must pay*.' Hilda's eyes grew wide.

'Then we searched Alexander Kratzenstein's desk in the train carriage,' Ozan said.

'But we didn't find the missing will,' Hal assured her.

'And after Hal and Herman were nearly killed—'

'We wouldn't have died,' Hal interrupted.

'You don't know that,' Ozan replied, enjoying the drama. 'Hilda, we went up on to the top of the pass and we found footprints. Then we saw Freya and Rada, so I followed them.' He turned to Hal, looking like he might burst with what he had to say. 'They rented a house in Wernigerode a month ago. They were *here* at the time Alexander died. Freya told Rada that she wished she had talked to her brother before he died. Then they discussed some *plan* they have, although they didn't say what it was.'

'Hilda,' Hal smiled sweetly at her. 'We're going to need your help if we are to make sense of any of this. You know so much about detecting.'

Hilda's glowering expression softened, her curiosity eclipsing her anger. 'Why are you holding a boot and a shoe?' she asked her brother.

'I followed Freya back to the house. She took her boots off and left them in the cloakroom.' He held up the boot. 'Look, it's too small to have made the footprints we found at the top of Dead Man's Pass.' He held up the shoe. 'But this shoe looks about the right size.'

'Hang on, I need my glasses,' Hal said, pulling out his pocketbook. He went to his bed and put them on, flipping the pocketbook so that they wouldn't see any of his other drawings, just the page with the two footprints. 'Put Freya's boot down on the floor.' Ozan did, and Hal put his foot beside it. Freya's boot was the same size as his. 'Now try the shoe.' Ozan lifted the boot and put down the shoe beside Hal's foot. Hal held out the drawing so they could all see it.

'The shoe does look roughly the same size as the footprint,' Hilda said, 'but it's hardly a match.'

'That's because the print was made by a boot still on the foot of the person who made it.' Ozan said, picking up the shoe and gave them a meaningful look. 'This is Aksel's shoe. I bet that print was made by Aksel's boot.'

'You think Aksel sent the stones crashing on to Hal and Herman?' Hilda looked alarmed.

'Yes. He's related to Gobel Babelin and taking her revenge,' Ozan said dramatically.

'Let's not jump to conclusions,' Hal said. 'I wonder why Freya hasn't she told anyone she was in Wernigerode when Alexander died?'

'And why is she making strange potions with wild plants and stream water –' Ozan looked at each of them – 'like a witch?'

'This is a real mystery,' Hilda said excitedly, 'and we're going to solve it!'

CHAPTER TWENTY-FOUR

CRYPTANALYSIS

'Hilda, can you help me?' Hal sat down on the bed opposite her.

'Is it about the case?' Hilda looked up from her journal, where Hal could see she'd been scribbling a list in German.

'No,' Hal said apologetically. 'I told my dad what you said about language being a type of code and he set me a puzzle.' Hal showed her the message he'd found hidden inside the rat. 'I think he wants me to decode it, but I don't know how.'

Hilda studied the page. 'Is this all he gave you?'

'Yes.'

'This looks like a cipher, rather than a code.' Seeing the puzzled look on his face, she explained. 'A cipher is when letters are encrypted separately. In a code, whole words are encrypted and can be represented by symbols or other things.' She looked back at the page. 'This is almost impossible to work out if you don't have the key. You could look for patterns, like repeated words or single letters. Look here.' She pointed. 'This N is on its own. N is probably an I or an A – they're the only letters in English that can be a whole word by themselves. And here and here, T2EO is repeated. But . . .' She shook her head. 'There are infinite possibilities.'

'Maybe that's the puzzle – I have to guess what the key is. What kinds of things can be keys?'

'A key can be anything that tells the writer and the reader which letters or numbers to swap in for the alphabet.' Her face lit up. 'Look, the message starts with a number: 3956-7.'

'What does that mean?'

'If a book is used as a key, a number at the start could indicate the page the key is taken from.' She frowned. 'But it would be a very large book if it had three thousand, nine hundred and fifty-six pages.' The excitement sluiced away as she realized that she couldn't be right. 'I don't know,' she said, handing back the pocketbook. 'I think your dad made the puzzle too hard. Why don't you ask him for a clue?'

'I think I will,' Hal said, walked as casually as he could to the tower door, but neither Hilda and Ozan showed a flicker of interest. They were both intent on being the first to solve the mystery of the curse.

When Hal got to Uncle Nat's bedroom door, he knocked and waited.

'Hello, Harrison.' Hilda and Ozan's dad was coming out of his room.

'Hello, Mr Essenbach. I'm looking for my dad. You haven't seen him, have you?'

'I saw him at breakfast, but then he went for a morning stroll. I'll bet he's joined the goat hunt. Did you hear? One of them has escaped the pen.' Oliver grinned. 'I would have helped, but Bertha has told me the location of the key to the private library.' He looked excited. 'I'm hoping to discover something that will shine a new light on *Faust*.'

'This mountain, the Brocken . . . That's in *Faust*, isn't it?'

Oliver nodded. 'It's a very interesting place.'

'Because of witches?'

'Not just witches. Stories tell of the flat summit being created by the stamp of a giant horse's hoof, and that a troop of ghastly huntsmen ride through the ancient forests. The Brocken is steeped in folklore. I think it is because of the weather.'

'The weather?'

'The Brocken is misty nearly all year. That's what causes the spectre.'

'There are ghosts here?'

'No.' Oliver laughed. 'The Brocken spectre is not a ghost— it's a weather phenomenon. If you climb to the summit and look down into the mist, with the sun behind you, your shadow is projected on to the cloud. The angle makes a giant moving ghost with a rainbow aura. Climbers throughout history have been literally terrified by their own shadows.'

'This place is so full of stories it's confusing –' Hal shook his head – 'and they all seem to be scary.'

'Its history is one of the reasons this place is so popular with tourists – and the ancient forest and wildlife,' Oliver conceded. 'The Brocken is the highest mountain of the Harz. In the Second World War, its television tower made it a target for Allied bombing.'

'It was bombed?'

'Yes. Then after the war the Russians came, and the Brocken became a security zone – a military fortress – because it was part of the border between East and West Germany. A concrete wall was built round the top of the mountain. No one was allowed up it. Border guards were stationed there. The Stasi – the East German secret police – turned the summit into a listening post, and the Soviet Red Army . . .'

Though Hal was interested in the history of the Brocken, it wasn't going to help him find the key to his cypher and so he interrupted. 'Mr Essenbach, what is so special about *Faust*? It seems to be about sly devils, farting witches and stinky goats?'

'Some of it is funny –' Oliver chuckled – 'but the play is a conversation between the devil and a man about the meaning of existence: the perils and flaws of being human. It has big truths in it. That's why it's an important story. "Each sees in the world what he holds in his heart." That's from the Prelude in the Theatre, line one hundred and seventy something, depending on the translation.'

'Because plays are made up of *lines*!' Hal exclaimed. 'Thank you, Mr Essenbach. You've been a great help.' He put his hand on the door handle.

'Glad to be of service,' Oliver said, looking confused.

'I'm going to leave a note for my dad,' Hal said. 'Enjoy the library.'

'Oh yes, I will.' Oliver nodded and walked away with a skip in his step.

The room was empty. Wherever Uncle Nat had gone after his visit to the station, he hadn't yet returned. Hal's eyes went straight to the nightstand. *Faust* was gone. He looked around the room. Then he saw it on the writing desk, in a stack with other books. Closing the door, he ran to the desk, sliding the book out and flicking through the pages. The piece of paper marking a page was gone. He saw tiny line numbers written in the margin of the pages. The play didn't have acts or scenes, *just lines*. He turned the pages till he found line 3956, took out his pocketbook and scribbled it and the next line down:

Up Brocken mountain witches fly,
When stubble is yellow and green the crop.

There was that mention of witches again. His heart was racing. He didn't want to get caught snooping, but he had to find out what the message said. Replacing the book in the pile, he ran back to the door, looked once around the room, making sure he hadn't disturbed anything, and stepped outside, checking the coast was clear.

Hurrying to the first door beyond the guest rooms, he found it was a linen cupboard with shelves of sheets and towels, and a pile of cleaning materials. Scurrying inside, he listened with his ear pressed against the wood for a second, then looked down at pocketbook. *He had the key!* Turning round, he saw a beady-eyed vulture perched on a bleached white branch bolted to the wall above the shelves, looking judgmental.

'What are you
looking at?'
Hal said
to the
vulture
as he sat
on the floor.

First, he wrote out
the alphabet, then underneath
it he wrote the sequential letters from the
lines of Faust. He flicked the page between the key and the
message.

A	B	C	D	E	F	G	H	I	J	K	L	M	N	O	P	Q	R	S	T	U	V	W	X	Y	Z
U	P	B	R	O	C	K	E	N	M	O_2	U_2	N_2	T	A	$I N_3$	WI_2	T_2	C_2	HE_2	S	F	L			

$3956-7$. $N_2OI_2I_2UKO$ WOBONHOR. $EUTKN_2UT$
$ROUBT_2NHUT_2OR$. NC AC_2W $RWNOR-C_2I$
$UI_2I_2OT_2$ $NI_2T'T_2$ $BAN_2IWAN_2NI_2OR$, N $E_2NU_2U_2$
I_2T_2UTR RAE_2T. T_2EO BUI_2O NI_2 ONT_2EOW
$TUT_2C_2WUU_2$ AW U $RAN_2OI_2T_2NB$ $BWNN_2O$.
T_2EO $XNKTUU_2N_2UT$

The first letter of the message was an N followed by a 2. He
frowned. There were no numbers in the key. What did 2 mean?
He looked at the key again and saw that there were three Ns.
He realized the number two indicated it was the second N in
the key, which would make it an M. Hal ran his finger along

the key until he came to the second N in the line, the N of *mountain*, and saw it was underneath M. He wrote down M on a fresh page. The next letter was O, which was an E.

'M . . . E . . .' he muttered.

He kept going, decoding the next letters as S, S, A, G . . .

'Message!' Hal whispered feeling a flash of excitement. He'd done it! He'd worked out the key. He decoded the rest of the message.

MESSAGE RECEIVED. HANGMAN DEACTIVATED. IF OUR DRIED-UP ASSET ISN'T COMPROMISED, I WILL STAND DOWN. THE CASE IS EITHER NATURAL OR A DOMESTIC CRIME.

THE SIGNALMAN

Hal stared at the paper. He had no idea what the message meant. There was that word HANGMAN again. It must have some special meaning. Hal guessed that THE CASE was a reference to Alexander Kratzenstein's mysterious death, but what was a DRIED-UP ASSET? And who was THE SIGNALMAN?

CHAPTER TWENTY-FIVE

THE SIGNALMAN

It dawned on Hal that he hadn't talked freely with Uncle Nat since Friday morning. Had his uncle purposefully been avoiding him? Was he the Signalman? The realization that he might not know his uncle as well as he thought he did shook him. He suddenly missed the comforting warmth of his mother's smile and the joyful face-licks of his dog, Bailey.

Looking down at the pocketbook, he felt a flush of guilt. He wanted to find his uncle, ask him all the questions buzzing in his head, but he couldn't do that without admitting he'd been investigating him. And then it occurred to him that in investigating his uncle he had been distracted from the mystery the baron had brought him here to solve.

Tucking his pocketbook away, Hal got to his feet, deciding that he should focus his attention on the dangers of Dead Man's Pass. Someone had sent a cascade of snow and rock down on him and Herman, and he'd almost forgotten the clue he'd discovered in the skull's nose.

Checking the coast was clear, he slipped out of the linen

cupboard. There was a circular gold-framed mirror hanging beside the wooden arch, and he stopped to look in it. He took off his glasses and flattened his fringe down.

'Come on, Hal,' he whispered to himself. 'Think. Something is going on in this house. Someone is up to no good. Who is it?'

Hearing a *clunk*, he hurriedly put his glasses on and withdrew into the shadows, peering along the corridor. Bertha emerged from the corridor that led to her rooms. Her eyes were swollen, and he wondered if it had been her he'd heard crying earlier. His mind flashed up the image of the paper sticking out of her desk drawer. Was it Alexander's missing will? Tiptoeing to the corner, he watched her disappear down the stairs to the kitchen.

There was only one way to find out what that piece of paper was, and this might be his only chance to look.

Creeping into Bertha's private living room, Hal ran to her desk drawer. The paper was no longer sticking out. He pulled at the drawer and found it was locked. The other drawers were unlocked, but contained no key. Whatever was in that drawer, Bertha didn't want people to see it. He scanned the room, running his fingers along the top of the window frame and searching in all the obvious places.

'If I were Bertha, where would I keep the key to my private papers?' Hal muttered to himself, trying to ignore his racing heart.

Then he thought of the family photo in her bedroom. It was the only personal item in her rooms. On a hunch, he scurried into the bedroom, and, going to her bedside table, he lifted the framed photograph and turned it round.

'Bingo!'

Taped to the back of the frame was a small silver key.

With shaking hands, he tried the key in the lock. It fitted. His ears strained for the *clickety-clack* of Bertha's footsteps as he opened the drawer. He felt a flare of triumph as he pulled out the wad of papers inside. But when he skimmed through them his triumph crumbled to ashes. He was holding well-worn hand-written pages, letters. They were written in German, so he couldn't read them, but each one was addressed to Bertha and signed by Alexander. The ink was blurred in places by spots of water, probably tears. There were kisses at the bottom of each letter. He hadn't found the missing will. These were love letters from a young Alexander to a young Bertha.

Carefully replacing them, Hal locked the drawer and taped the key to the back of the picture frame again, his insides burning with shame. He ran into the bedroom, desperate to get out of there. He put it down clumsily and it fell over with a clunk. He stood it back up and edged out of the room and into the corridor.

'Hal?' His uncle's voice made him jump. 'What are you doing?' Hal spun round. There was a judgmental look on Uncle Nat's face.

'What are *you* doing, more like?' he blurted out. '*Signalman.*' Immediately shocked that he'd said it, Hal held his breath.

Uncle Nat stiffened, then checked over his shoulder, making sure no one had heard. 'Come with me.' He calmly

193

put a hand on Hal's back and guided him back along the corridor.

Entering his uncle's room, Hal was certain he was in big trouble.

Uncle Nat picked up the desk chair and placed it next to the basin in the corner of the room. 'Sit down.' He put his finger to his lips, to show Hal should be silent, and went and closed the door. Returning, he turned the taps on full so that the water ran gurgling into the plughole. Perching on the corner of the bed, he leaned forward so that his head was close to Hal's. 'I would like you to tell me what you know,' he said in a quiet, serious voice.

Hal swallowed. 'I saw you at the station.' He matched his voice to his uncle's tone. 'I found the message in the rat.'

Uncle Nat drew in a long breath. 'Did you remove it?'

'No. I copied it and put it back.'

'Excellent.' Uncle Nat nodded. 'Well done.'

'Why are the taps running?' Hal glanced at the sink.

'I'm using the running water as interference, in case anyone is listening to us.'

Hal looked at the door in alarm. 'Who would be listening?' He felt a shiver of fear.

'Have you told anyone about the message?'

Hal shook his head.

'Good.' Uncle Nat pushed his glasses up his nose, pausing to think. 'Hal, I'm going to tell you something that is a secret, a grown-up secret. But, before I do, I must ask you to promise not to tell anyone, ever. Not even your mum and dad.'

The hairs on the back of Hal's neck rose. 'I promise.'

'Thank you.' His eyes wandered as he considered how to begin. 'Some time ago, I was what they call . . . a birdwatcher.'

'A birdwatcher?'

'An intelligence officer. I worked for the Secret Intelligence Service, gathering and transporting intelligence – information. My code name was the Signalman. My job as a travel journalist was a convenient cover, allowing me to connect with operatives all over the world.'

Hal stared at his uncle. 'You were a spy?'

'Yes,' said Uncle Nat, meeting his eyes. 'I was a spy.'

CHAPTER TWENTY-SIX

A BIRDWATCHER

'It was a long time ago,' Uncle Nat explained, 'back when you were very little.'

'How did you become a spy?'

'I was recruited at university. I spoke several languages. I liked travel. It seemed like an interesting job at the time.'

'Then why did you give it up?'

Uncle Nat smiled. 'I fell in love. My priorities changed when I met James.'

'The baron knows you were a spy!' Hal realized. 'That's why he wrote to you.'

'He wrote to *us* because he didn't understand what was happening here, and one of the things he was concerned about relates to my old job. He hoped I could look into it.'

'HANGMAN,' Hal said.

'Yes. Hangman.'

'What does it mean?'

'It's a coded alert used when the life of an agent, or an asset, is in danger.'

'But Alexander was already dead . . .' Hal's brain made a series of connections, and he suddenly saw the truth. 'It wasn't Alexander the baron was worried about, was it? It was Arnold. He's the dried-up asset in the message.'

'How did you work that out?'

'There's a red lantern in the topmost window of the tower. Arnold turns it on using his model trains. Last night, when you went out in the snow, the lantern was on. I noticed the red light behind Arnie when he'd played his trick on us with the bat. The red light is a signal.'

Uncle Nat looked impressed. 'It's a signal that a communication is being made.'

'A signal to who? Arnold's spy contacts?'

'During the Cold War, Arnold was an informant. His railway lines were the backbone of the Soviet Union's presence here, so he knew a lot about what they were doing. He lived and worked in East Germany, but he shared valuable secrets with the West. After the reunification of Germany, he no longer needed to do it, and retired.' Uncle Nat shook his head. 'This was long before you were born, but if the wrong people found out what he did back then his life could be in danger now. They would see him as a traitor.'

'Arnold thinks Alexander was killed by mistake because someone was after *him*.'

Uncle Nat nodded. 'He called the baron because he thought his life, and those of the people living here, were in danger.'

'Is the baron a spy?'

'No, the baron is an ally. In the past, he's provided safe houses and helped operatives in trouble.'

'Do spies really leave each other messages inside dead rats?' Hal wrinkled his nose. 'It's not very glamorous.'

'It's called a *dead drop*.' Uncle Nat chuckled. 'It's a way for agents to leave messages for each other when it's not safe for them to meet. In Berlin, I visited an old friend who told me how to contact an agent in Wernigerode – someone who'd know about Arnold having been exposed as an informant. The local agent I've been communicating with, through the dead drop, is only known to me as Arctic Fox. They've assured me this is not a Hangman situation – Arnold's life is not in danger.'

'You think Alexander died naturally, or his death was a domestic crime,' Hal said, repeating the message.

'Yes, but I'm curious. Tell me, how did you know how to decode the message?'

'I spotted HANGMAN in the baron's letter in Paris, and then I realized that *Faust* was the key to the code because it was the book he recommended that you buy.' Hal didn't admit that without Hilda's help he would never have worked it out.

'Ha!' Uncle Nat sat back. 'Thank goodness most humans aren't as observant as you.'

'Is an asset the same as a birdwatcher?' Hal asked, groping with the terminology.

'No. An asset is a person who gathers information to pass on, or disseminates false information. They stay in one place. A birdwatcher travels.'

Hal looked at his uncle. 'Did you like being a spy?'

'Not enough to keep being one,' Uncle Nat replied. 'But enough about me. What about you? How have your investigations been going?'

'The baron is right – there is something strange going on here,' Hal said. 'But I can't work out who is behind it or why.' He told his uncle about finding the commonplace book with the turned-down page, the incident of the rocks falling on to the sledge and about Aksel's locket and the strange comment he'd made about the Kratzensteins. 'I've looked everywhere for the missing will, but I haven't found it. Ozan overheard Freya and Rada saying they were here, in Wernigerode, when Alexander died, and they're planning something, but we don't know what.'

'Freya was here?' Uncle Nat was startled.

'Yes, and she's picking lots of strange plants. She's got a weird copper cauldron in her room that she told me she uses for making potions.' Hal looked at his uncle meaningfully.

'And you think . . . ?'

'Well, she's got a black cat and a cauldron . . .' Hal started to say, and Uncle Nat laughed. 'What?'

'Freya is a very successful perfumier. She lives in Cologne and has a laboratory of people making exclusive perfumes for those who can afford them. She's known for having a nose for unusual blends of scent. I guess you could call her perfumes *potions*.' He paused. 'But it's strange that she was in Wernigerode when Alexander died. I wonder what she was doing here.'

'Could Freya have a reason to get rid of the missing will?'

'She has enough money of her own, so unless she's interested in a controlling share of K-Bahn – which I doubt she is – I don't think so. Alexander left everything to Clara and Herman, which makes Bertha and Arnie suspects.'

'Bertha loved Alexander.'

'Once, but she had an argument with him the night he died. She was angry that he'd hired Connie to look after Arnold. She thought he was trying to push her out of Schloss Kratzenstein, and she was probably right.'

'No, Bertha would never have killed Alexander,' Hal said, thinking of the love letters she kept locked away in her desk.

'There doesn't seem to be anyone who wanted Alexander dead.' Uncle Nat shook his head. 'That's why I think it must have been a normal heart attack.'

Hal smiled. 'It's nice to be able to talk theories through with you. It's hard pretending to be Harrison Strom. I don't like lying to Ozan, Hilda and Herman. They're nice. It must have been difficult being a spy.'

'It was lonely,' Uncle Nat replied, and Hal nodded, feeling closer to his uncle now they shared a secret. 'But you won't have to pretend for much longer. Tomorrow is the funeral, which will be a difficult day, but on Tuesday morning, we'll catch a train back to Berlin and go home. I promised your mother I'd get you home before Easter.' Uncle Nat smiled. 'The moment we step on to that train, we can drop the disguises.'

'Then I only have thirty-six hours to solve the mystery of how Alexander Kratzenstein died,' Hal said.

CHAPTER TWENTY-SEVEN

THE FUNERAL TRAIN

The next morning, snow lay thick on the ground and, although fresh flakes had stopped falling, a white fog hung in the air. Hal got dressed in his black trousers and jacket for the funeral and followed Herman, Hilda and Ozan down to breakfast.

Going to the platform doorway of the salon, Hal paused to watch Aksel working as the others filed into the dining room. The vintage black-and-red Class 99 tank engine was sitting in a cloud of steam at the head of the funeral train. Behind it was the sombre carriage, in which Alexander Kratzenstein lay in his coffin, and behind that were two empty wooden carriages awaiting the funeral guests.

'Morning.' Hal walked up to Aksel as he opened a hatch in the top of the boiler and fed in the water hose. Aksel nodded. 'Is the train ready?'

Aksel pointed to the snowplough bolted to the front of the locomotive.

'He's been working on the train for hours,' said Connie,

who was wrapped in her coat and watching Aksel with affectionate interest from further along the plaform. 'He wants to make sure the engine has enough water to get her up the mountain and back again.'

'It's very important a loco doesn't run out of water.' Hal nodded. 'If the water runs out, the engine can explode.'

'Really?' Connie stared at the engine. 'That sounds terribly dangerous.'

'It's like a giant kettle that keeps on boiling after all the water's evaporated. But don't worry,' Hal said, seeing the concern on her face. 'Aksel knows what he's doing.'

*

A few hours later, a line of cars struggled up the snowy drive to Schloss Kratzenstein. Hilda, Ozan and Hal were sitting on the floor of the gallery, looking down on the ballroom where the guests were being welcomed by the willowy Clara Kratzenstein. Her long blonde hair was loose, and she wore a floaty black silk dress, with sleeves that ended at her elbows, long lace cuffs stretching to her delicate wrists. Her skin was ghostly pale, her blue eyes shone with tears. Hal could see why Alexander Kratzenstein had fallen in love with her.

'I fear the snow may prevent many of the funeral guests from travelling,' the baron said to Uncle Nat. 'It will be a small gathering.'

'The size of the gathering is not important,' Clara said, dabbing her eyes with a black lace handkerchief.

When the doctor and his wife arrived, they were greeted warmly by Bertha in her smart black suit.

'Look, that's Marie Winkelmann,' Hilda whispered, pointing at a frail-looking woman. 'She's a distant relative of the Count of Wernigerode.'

'Why is she here?' Hal asked.

'She was Manfred Kratzenstein's fiancée. He died before they could get married.'

Bertha was striding about, informing people there was coffee and cake for them on a long table to the side of the room. Arnie was standing beside the table, looking longingly at the silver platter of cake slices.

'Mmm, *Zuckerkuchen*,' Ozan murmured.

'It's a cake we have at funerals,' Hilda explained. 'It's sweet and buttery.'

'Poor Herman,' Hal said, watching a man bend to talk down to him. 'I wouldn't want to talk to anyone if this was my dad's funeral.'

'That man is probably being kind,' Hilda said.

'That's worse,' Hal replied. 'It would make me cry.'

'We should go down,' Ozan said, and Hilda got to her feet as Hal and Ozan stood up and dusted off their trousers.

'I've never been to a funeral before,' Hal admitted.

'They're boring.' Ozan pulled a face. 'And seeing adults cry is weird.'

'Adults don't know how to let their tears out,' Hilda agreed. 'They try to hold them back and end up making noises like hedgepigs.'

'Hedge*hogs*,' Hal corrected her, with a chuckle.

Filing down the stairs, they joined the fringe of the group in the ballroom, and Hal found himself surrounded by soft, respectful conversations in German. Hilda translated for him in whispers. 'That's Herr Gotthold.' She pointed with her nose at the man Clara was talking to. 'He's the Mayor of Wernigerode. He's offering his condolences.'

Hal saw the doctor slip out of the hall and decided to follow him. He had a question he wanted to ask the man. He found him outside the back door, standing in the kitchen garden, puffing on a pipe.

'Hello.' Hal shook the surprised doctor's hand. 'I'm Harrison.'

'Herr Melchior.'

'Are you the doctor?'

Herr Melchior nodded.

'You did the autopsy on Alexander Kratzenstein?'

The doctor dropped his chin, looking at Hal over his gold-rimmed spectacles in surprise.

'You believe the cause of his death to be a heart attack?'

'I do not believe, I *know* he died of a heart attack, and I would not use the word *cause* in this way.'

'What might cause a heart attack?'

'A shock, perhaps . . .' The doctor paused. 'Or some bad news.' He turned his pipe upside down and tapped it against the wall, emptying its contents on to the snow. 'A fright causes the body's fight-or-flight mechanism to flood the system with adrenalin. Adrenalin can trigger a heart attack and there was whisky in his bloodstream.'

'Do you think Mr Kratzenstein was frightened?'

'Alexander wasn't the kind of man to jump at shadows.' The doctor fell silent, staring at nothing, and then whispered, 'He looked terrified.' He shook his head. 'It was so strange. He had a white substance on his fingertips, a chalky paint. It was on his shirt collar too – probably from when he tried to undo his shirt collar.'

Hal thought about the white face paint he'd found in the skull's nose. 'He tried to undo his shirt?'

'This is not a conversation for a child,' the doctor said, patting Hal's head. He slipped his pipe into his jacket pocket. 'Come, let us return to the party.'

Following the doctor back into the hall, Hal stepped sideways and sat on a chair inside the door, pulling out his pocketbook and pen. He let his mind go blank and began to draw.

The grieving widows, Clara and Bertha, both with sons they loved fiercely and a claim on Alexander's estate, circled old Arnold in his wheelchair. Connie stood against the wall, dressed in a plain black dress, her short blonde hair tucked neatly behind her ears, a blanket over her arm, should Arnold need it to warm his legs. Freya was wearing a charcoal dress under a frockcoat with a high collar and ruffles round the hem. Her hair was piled up like a Victorian lady's and she was holding Belladonna in her arms. Rada stood next to her,

looking striking in a black trouser suit, her hair covered by a black headwrap knotted above her forehead. Uncle Nat was talking with the Mayor and the baron. Arnie and Ozan were standing either side of the platter of funeral cake, eating. Hilda had her hand through Herman's arm. He was staring into space like a zombie.

Aksel entered the room dressed in a suit, and at first Hal didn't recognize him. He'd washed the dirt from his hands and face, slicked his hair back, tying it in a ponytail, and his beard was trimmed. He approached Bertha and whispered something to her. Bertha nodded, and went to stand beside Arnold.

'*Freunde, es ist Zeit für uns alle in den Zug einzusteigen. Bitte*

folgt mir,' Bertha said, and turned towards the doorway where Hal was sitting drawing. He jumped up, hiding his pen and pocketbook behind his back, as she strode towards him, and everyone calmly followed her through the house.

Hal fell in step beside Uncle Nat. 'I talked to the doctor,' he whispered. 'He thinks something caused Alexander's heart attack.' He paused. 'If someone frightened him on purpose . . . is that murder?'

'If you wanted to kill someone, there are simpler, more effective ways of doing it,' Uncle Nat replied.

The funeral train was waiting for them in Kratzenstein Halt.

To Hal's surprise, Arnold got up out of his wheelchair and boarded with assistance from Arnie. Bertha, Clara and Herman followed him. Freya handed Belladonna to Rada, before boarding the carriage and closing the door. Rada put Belladonna into her basket as Connie folded Arnold's wheelchair, and both women went into the second carriage with the other guests.

'Isn't this wonderfully creepy?' Hilda whispered to Hal as she and Ozan followed their dad on to the train.

'We want to be at the back,' Uncle Nat said under his breath, gently putting his hand on Hal's shoulder as he moved to follow Hilda. 'We can stand outside on the veranda at the end of the train as it travels up the mountainside.' Hal looked at his uncle, surprised. 'One should be respectful at funerals, but there's no rule that says you're not allowed to enjoy yourself,' Uncle Nat said. 'Alexander loved trains. He would have approved.'

They got into the third carriage and Hal followed his uncle out on to the veranda.

The locomotive let out a long, sorrowful whistle as it pulled away from Kratzenstein Halt, towing the sombre train through the archway, past the train shed and the goat pen towards Dead Man's Pass.

'Did you find the missing goat?'

'No, I fear it may have met with a mishap,' Uncle Nat replied as the train approached the cutting. 'There are wolves on the mountain.'

'See the nose hole in the skull?' Hal pointed. 'I found a cloth bag in there with white and black face paint in it.'

Uncle Nat looked at him sharply.

'And there are candle stubs and pools of dried wax in the eye sockets. I think it's a clue. The doctor said Alexander had white paint on his fingers.'

The two of them stared silently at the macabre visage of the skull as they passed by.

When the funeral train joined the Brockenbahn, clunking over the points, Hal exchanged a smile with his uncle as they passed through the station with the dead drop. At a red-and-white level crossing, a crowd of people had gathered. The train approached and some removed their hats as a mark of respect. The loco blasted out a mournful whistle and everyone on both sides of the tracks bowed their heads, as Alexander Kratzenstein passed by on his final train journey.

Winding up the mountainside, through the Harz national

park, Hal saw frozen spider webs strung between trees, frost hair sprouting from branches, and crystalline patches of treacherous ice. At each bend and corner, the whistle wailed.

As they climbed towards the peak, the trees grew thinner and the snow thicker. The orange-and-white spike of the listening tower rose above the line of trees, piercing the clouds, its flashing red light mirroring the red signal in Arnold's tower. Mist drifted through the trees, like slow waltzing spectres. The plumes of powder-grey smoke exhaled by the tank engine seemed to thicken the low clouds that hid the sun. Hal felt like the funeral train was travelling out of this world to a station somewhere between the living and the dead.

They pulled into a siding, past cut-back foliage, to a short platform of wooden planks the length of a carriage. The train halted so the double doors in the centre of the first carriage were beside the platform. Aksel climbed down from the footplate to open the doors. Uncle Nat jumped down from the veranda, hurrying to help Connie, who was wrestling with the folded wheelchair. Arnie and Aksel each pulled back one of the double doors, and Hal saw the black coffin on a plinth in the carriage, surrounded by white flowers.

Clara and Herman got off the train, holding hands, and Bertha followed them, her arm a prop for Arnold to lean on.

Hal went to stand beside Hilda and Ozan, and the three of them watched as the baron, Aksel, Arnie, Freya, Oliver Essenbach and Dr Melchior went and stood around the coffin. The baron said something quietly, and each of them gripped a silver handle. He muttered again, and the six of them lifted the coffin in unison. Herman went to stand with Arnold, who took his hand. As the coffin was lifted from the train, the pair went in front of it, soundlessly leading the procession along the path through the trees to a white stone building wreathed in ivy.

Hal followed the procession, keeping his eyes on the ground, listening to the creak of footsteps on snow. Creeping fingers of cold walked up his spine, and he shivered at the sound of crows cawing in the canopy above.

The Kratzenstein mausoleum was built into the side of the mountain, its facade a white stone arch over a door topped by a cross on a pedestal. A pastor in religious robes was standing beside the door.

Inside, the mausoleum resembled a miniature church and was filled with flowers. Hal went and stood with Uncle Nat at the back of the room. It was so cold he could see his breath.

The service began, but it was in German, and Hal struggled to understand anything but the name of the dead man. Freya got up and said something that sounded like a poem. Arnold said some words, and poor Clara was too tearful to get out a whole sentence.

Hal was studying the guests, wishing he could take out his pocketbook, when a strange high-pitched noise lifted all the hairs on his body.

'*Blut! Da ist Blut an meinen Händen!*' Herman wailed.

Uncle Nat jumped to his feet. Aksel stepped forward from the back of the room.

Hal rose too. 'What did he say?'

But before Uncle Nat could answer, Arnie, who was in the adjacent front pew to Herman, cried out in fear and anguish. He held up his hands, and Hal could see that they were dripping with blood.

'They have blood on their hands!' Aksel growled.

CHAPTER TWENTY-EIGHT

MAELSTROM

People gasped, crying out fearfully and jumping to their feet. The funeral erupted. Clara stood with her arms round Herman, who held his blood-stained hands away from his face as he wailed hysterically. Arnie was shouting, '*Wer hat das gemacht? Wer von euch hat mir das angetan?*'

Uncle Nat rushed to the baron's side. Hal pulled out his pocketbook and, lightning fast, drew as many vignettes as he could, capturing the information from the scene in front of him.

The man conducting the service was trying to calm everybody down, but the Mayor, Marie Winkelmann and many of the guests who weren't family

213

were fleeing the mausoleum. Hal could hear the chatter outside: '*Es war die Hexe . . .*' '*Die Hexe hat das getan . . .*'

Dr Melchior was beside Arnie, examining his hands. He confirmed to the baron that it was real blood.

Connie was helping a confused and frail-looking Arnold into his wheelchair, tucking his blanket over his knees. She was trying to calm him down, but he kept trying to get up.

Freya and Rada's heads were bent towards one another. They were deep in conversation, oblivious to the commotion around them.

Hilda had rushed to Herman's aid. She had a handkerchief and was wiping Herman's hands. She poured water from a bottle, rinsing them and drying them with the sleeve of her coat.

Herman looked stunned and was shaking. Hal felt anger burning in his chest. Someone in this room was terrifying Herman on purpose. And, despite Arnie's bluster and his pretending to be a grown-up, Hal could see that he was scared too.

Clara, who had been talking to Connie, turned to Arnold and said something in German. She looked like she was pleading with him.

'*Nein*,' Arnold replied gruffly with a shake of his head. 'I've lived all my life on this mountain. I will never leave. I don't want to live in Berlin.'

The baron spoke to Aksel and the pastor, who turned and held up his arms, quieting the chatter. He said something in German, then he, the baron, Uncle Nat, Aksel, Arnie and Oliver lifted the coffin and solemnly carried it to the back of the mausoleum and disappeared down a staircase. The pastor returned and spoke again. There were affirmative mutterings as people made their way out of the chapel. A few minutes later, Uncle Nat and the others returned.

'You OK?' Uncle Nat glanced down at the pocketbook, and Hal nodded. 'Funeral's over. We're getting the train back to the house. In light of these strange happenings, the dinner has been cancelled.'

'Where did the blood come from?'

'A nasty trick. Someone tipped blood into Herman and Arnold's gloves.'

'Who would do that?' Hal asked, appalled.

Uncle Nat shook his head. 'And why?'

The journey down the mountain seemed faster than the ascent. Hal sat inside with Uncle Nat and a carriage full of whispering guests.

Once the train had pulled into Kratzenstein Halt, everyone was eager to get away. They shook hands with Arnold, offered their condolences, returned to their parked vehicles out front and drove away.

Hal hovered in the salon, beside the suit of armour, watching the comings and goings of people like an eagle. Through the double doors, he could see Aksel on the platform. Freya and Rada were talking to him with serious expressions on their faces. He pointed to the train sheds.

Connie was clucking and fussing over Arnold, who was sitting in his wheelchair, glowering.

Hilda and Ozan had taken Herman off to have a bath, in the hope that it would make him feel better. The baron, Uncle Nat and Oliver Essenbach were in the dining room, talking in low, hushed voices. Alma was trying to keep Clara and Bertha from arguing with each other, as they each claimed the other was responsible for the stunt in the mausoleum. They were arguing in German, but Clara kept pointing angrily at Bertha, whose chin was raised, her expression defiant.

'What are you doing?' It was Arnie.

'Watching everyone.'

'Why?'

'I'm trying to work out who played that horrible trick on you and Herman.'

'You think it was someone in the family?'

'I don't know,' Hal admitted. 'I can't understand German. I don't know what they're all saying.'

'Clara is blaming Mama, saying she's been trying to get rid of her since they arrived. Mama is angry, outraged that Clara thinks she would do something like that to me.' He looked to his grandfather. 'Connie is trying to persuade Opa to take his medication.'

'Do you know what they're talking about?' Hal pointed through the dining-room doorway.

'The will. After the funeral, that is when you read the will, but Papa's will is missing.'

'You know about the missing will?'

'Of course.' Arnie grinned and lowered his voice. 'Mama burned it.'

'What?'

'Once Herr Melchior had proclaimed Papa dead, Mama went upstairs and locked herself in the study. She opened Opa's safe. She's known the combination for years. She took out Papa's will, read it, cried and then burned it on the fire. I watched her through the keyhole of the door in the music room.' He looked over at his mother. 'She was trying to protect me.'

Freya and Rada came back in and Hal saw that Rada had a plastic sleeve of paper under her arm. He spotted the logo of the three mountains. They approached the arguing women, and spoke with them in low tones.

'Aunt Freya's saying they should all go into the dining

room. They need to talk,' Arnie translated. 'C'mon, let's listen. This sounds interesting.'

The adults went into the dining room and closed the doors behind them.

'We'll never hear anything through those doors,' Hal said. 'They're really thick.'

'No, here. Upstairs. Come on.' Arnie bounded up the stairs two at a time, and Hal followed him into Arnold's model railway room. 'Here,' whispered Arnie, waving Hal over to the tunnel entrance that the trains travelled down to get to the dining-room table. They lowered their heads to the tunnel and Hal could hear everything, but everyone was speaking in German.

'I don't understand. Translate for me.'

Arnie waved at him to be quiet.

'Rada is talking. She is a lawyer. She says that as the will is missing, the family must decide how it wants to proceed. Mama is saying that she would have contested the will, as it disinherited me. She says that I have rights.' Arnie raised his eyebrows. 'Rada says that, as his spouse, Clara is legally entitled to a quarter of his estate, and that the rest is to be split equally between me and Herman.' He listened for a prolonged period and Hal studied his face, trying to work out what was going on.

'What are they saying?'

'If they split Papa's estate this way, I would own a share of the apartment in Berlin. Mama is trying to get Clara to agree to exchange the shares in K-Bahn that she would inherit, for my share in the apartment. Rada is saying that if the women can come to an agreement about the inheritance between them, and if there isn't another claim, then they could settle out of court. Opa thinks this is the best idea.' He blinked. 'Mama is saying that she and I are planning to move to Berlin and that Papa created a job for me at K-Bahn before he died.' He looked delighted. 'First I know of it!' But then something drew his head back to the tunnel, and he frowned, leaning right in. His body went rigid as he listened. He turned to Hal, looking shocked.

'What? What is it?'

Arnie didn't reply. He was still listening, but his expression darkened and grew angry.

'What's happening?'

Suddenly Arnold was surging towards him. He grabbed Hal by the scruff of the neck and pushed him against the wall. '*Du warst es!*'

Hal felt a bolt of panic as Arnold's hand wrapped round his neck. 'What are you doing? What's going on?'

'You English,' Arnold spat. 'You think you're so clever.'

'I don't understand!'

'Aunt Freya and Rada worked out your father's ugly scheme. They discovered the papers in Papa's desk. Was it you who put the blood in my gloves, you little English?' Arnie poked the side of Hal's face aggressively. 'You are broken in the head.'

'*WHAT?*' Hal felt the shock of these words like a bucket of icy water. 'I didn't! I . . .'

'They know.' He pointed at the tunnel. 'Rada has your father's letters to my papa.' Arnold let go of him and stepped back. 'You better go downstairs and say goodbye. The police are downstairs, and they are arresting your father *right now*.'

CHAPTER TWENTY-NINE

SPANNER IN
THE WORKS

Hal threw himself down the stairs at a breakneck speed, but when he arrived the dining room was empty. He pelted through the house to the grand entrance. The front door was wide open. He saw white cars with flashing blue lights and *Polizei* on the side. The baron was talking with a police officer. Freya and Rada were getting into one of the cars with Belladonna. Uncle Nat was already sitting in the back of one with Oliver Essenbach. His head turned, and he saw Hal. Hal tried to shout, but he didn't know whether to cry 'Dad' or 'Uncle Nat' and suddenly the cars were pulling away.

'Harrison.' Alma gently put her hand on his shoulder.

'What's happening? Why have they got my . . . dad?'

'Nathaniel asked me to look after you while he helps the police with their enquiries.' She turned him round. 'Let's go to the tower and find Hilda and Ozan.'

As Alma guided him back into the house, Clara and Bertha came out of the library, glaring coldly at him, finally united by their disdain for Uncle Nat.

'What happened?' Hal asked Alma.

'Freya believes your father and Alexander were trying to get Arnold to sell this house and the land. She says she has evidence that proves it. His signature is on letters to Alexander about the matter.' Alma corralled him into the lift and pressed the button for the tower. 'I'm sure there's an explanation for everything. Wolfgang will take care of it. Now I must get back to Clara and Bertha. I think it best you stay in the tower with Hilda and Ozan for now.'

Hal stepped out, turning to thank her, but the lift doors had closed.

'What's going on?' Ozan asked from the turret window. 'We saw the *Polizei*.'

'Are you OK?' Hilda was in a seat by the fire.

'Where's Herman?' Hal asked.

Ozan pointed to a curled-up lump in Herman's bed.

'He fell asleep after the bath,' Hilda said softly. 'Today was too much for him.'

'Good.' Hal ran up the spiral stairs, went to the window, reached into the model railway tunnel, switching on the red signal, then returned downstairs. He sat down on the edge of Hilda's bed, taking off his glasses. 'I need to tell you both something.'

Ozan and Hilda came and sat down opposite him, immediately interested.

'I am not who you think I am,' Hal said. 'I'm not related to you or Herman. I've been lying to you.' He watched their expressions change. 'My name is Harrison, and I do live in Crewe, but everything else is made up. My surname is not Strom, it's Beck.' Hilda opened her mouth to say something, then closed it. 'The man I call dad is not Nathan Strom. His name is Nathaniel Bradshaw, and I am not his son – I'm his nephew.'

'We're not cousins?' Ozan looked confused.

Hal shook his head. "We're not related, but I hope we are friends.'

Ozan leaned back as if seeing Hal for the first time.

'My uncle and I, we are . . . detectives. Your grandfather asked us to come, to investigate the strange occurrences surrounding Herman's dad's death. He didn't want to involve the police. It was his idea that we disguise ourselves as distant relatives.'

'You are detectives?' Ozan asked.

'Oh!' Hilda jumped to her feet and said to her brother. 'He's the railway detective boy! The one Opa told us solved the jewel-thief mystery on that steam train.'

'Yes. That's me.'

'That's why you're always scribbling in your journal,' Hilda exclaimed. 'You're not writing – you're drawing!'

'Drawing helps me think.'

'Why are you telling us this now?' Ozan asked.

'Because I need your help. My uncle has been arrested and I think we all might be in danger.'

Hilda gasped.

'Freya and Rada think they've found evidence that proves

my uncle is scheming to buy this house. Ozan, do you remember those papers we found in Alexander's desk in the train carriage? Well, Bertha found them too, and thought they were from my uncle.'

'But why might we be in danger?' Hilda said, glancing at the sleeping Herman.

'Because whoever put the blood in those gloves and sent rocks down on our sledge is still here.' He looked from Hilda to Ozan. 'We must all be detectives now.'

'What should we do?' Ozan said, seeing Hilda's alarmed expression.

'First, we need to get Arnold to tell us the truth about Frau Babelin's curse.'

'What are we waiting for?' Hilda jumped to her feet.

'Harrison,' Ozan whispered as they hurried down the stairs, 'what if putting the blood in the gloves and framing your uncle is all part of Freya and Rada's plan?'

'But why? What motive could Freya have?'

'I don't know . . . perhaps because they're witches too?' Ozan guessed.

'Freya is not a witch – she's a perfumier,' Hal said, 'and whoever put the blood in Herman's gloves is a cold and calculating person.'

At the bottom of the stairs, Hal put his finger to his lips as they tiptoed into the corridor that linked the family rooms. Loud rock music was blaring through the door of Arnie's room and Hal grimaced, thinking of how angry Arnie was with him.

Knocking gently at old Arnold's door, they waited, but

there was no answer. Hal tried again, putting his ear to the door, but he heard nothing. Taking a deep breath, Hal twisted the handle and opened the door.

The large room was divided in two. One half was a living room where a unfinished jigsaw lay on a table, and beyond were the double doors that led though to the room of model trains. The other half was Arnold's bedroom. Arnold's wheelchair was parked beside a four-poster bed, and the old man was lying in it, his eyes closed.

'What now?' Ozan whispered.

'We wake him up,' Hal said, walking over to the bed. He cleared his throat. 'Excuse me, Mr Kratzenstein.' There was no response. Hal leaned over and shook his arm. 'Mr Kratzenstein? Arnold?' The old man's head lolled to one side, but he didn't wake, and Hal felt a lash of fear.

'Is he . . . dead?' Ozan whispered.

'No.' Hilda shook a pot of pills on the bedside table. 'He's sedated, look. He's breathing.'

Hal was so relieved to see the old man's chest rise and fall that his legs went to jelly. He leaned on the wheelchair to steady himself.

'We can't question someone who is unconscious,' said Ozan. 'What now?' He wandered over to the window. 'Hey, it's started snowing again.'

Hal came and stood beside Ozan as tiny specks of snow drifted past the glass at a dreamlike pace. 'Why is the train still there?' He looked down at the halt. 'I thought Aksel was putting it away.'

'Look – boots.' Ozan pointed to a rack by the door. He went and picked up the left foot of a pair of walking boots. 'Have you still got that drawing of the footprint in the snow?'

Hal took out his pocketbook and the photograph of the Stroms that the baron had included in his dossier fluttered to the floor. He picked it up as Ozan put Arnold's boot beside his foot. They considered the difference in size, then turned the boot over to see the underside. The sole had the same markings as the footprint.

'We have a match,' Ozan said.

'But Arnold can't have climbed to the top of Dead Man's Pass,' Hilda protested.

'Can't he?' Ozan said. 'We all saw him walking at the funeral.'

They all turned and looked at the sleeping man.

'It could be hours before he wakes up,' Hilda said. 'We should ask Connie how long the sedative lasts.'

'Good idea,' Hal said, leaving the room and knocking on the door opposite. But there was no answer. 'Where is everyone?' he muttered, turning the handle and pushing the door open.

'Are you sure this is hers?' Hilda asked, as the three of them stared at the empty room. The bed was made. The surfaces were clear of possessions.

Hal went to the wardrobe. Inside were hangers, but no clothes. He opened a door, which led to a bathroom. There was no toothbrush on the sink.

He looked at the others. 'She's gone!'

'Do you think the curse scared her away?' Hilda asked.

'She said she'd leave after the funeral,' replied Hal, 'but I didn't realize she meant this quickly.' He thought about the sweet nurse who'd warned him to leave Schloss Kratzenstein, then looked at the photo he was clutching and everything clicked into place. 'Who do you think hired Connie to look after Arnold?' he asked Hilda and Ozan as he hurried towards the stairs.

'Bertha,' said Hilda, at the same time as Ozan said, 'Alexander.' They stopped and stared at each other.

'She came here six months ago to look after Arnold,' Hal said, taking the stairs two at a time, 'but does anyone know where she was before that?'

'Bertha must know,' Hilda said. 'She would have interviewed the nurses. There must have been references.'

'Except Alma told me that Bertha was upset because Alexander had hired Connie to look after Arnold. She felt she was being pushed out of the family.'

'Yes, it was Alexander who hired her,' Ozan said. 'I heard that.'

'But Clara said it was Bertha who'd hired Connie, and that Alexander had been cross about it.'

'Then who did hire Connie?' Hilda squeaked, looking alarmed.

'No one,' Hal said, sprinting through the salon, and out on to the platform, where the funeral train was still standing. 'And Arnold couldn't have climbed Dead Man's Pass, but Connie had access to his boots.'

'Slow down,' Ozan gasped, catching up to Hal who had stopped and was staring at the train.

'That train should not be there,' he said. 'Aksel was going to put it away. Where is he?'

The children searched the courtyard, calling Aksel's name.

'His rooms are across the tracks.' Ozan pointed. 'He lives above the sheds.'

They ran round the engine, which was squirting out little jets of steam, and banged on the door to Aksel's room. There was no answer. They shouted up at the windows, but they were dark, and no lights came on.

'Do you think Aksel knows where Connie is?' Ozan asked.

'They could be together,' Hilda said. 'Remember his locket?'

'This isn't getting us anywhere,' Hal said, frustrated. 'Let's check the train shed.'

They hurried along the tracks, snow swirling in their faces. It was beginning to get dark, and Hal saw a lantern on in the workshop.

'There he is!' Ozan pointed, and they all saw a figure dressed in a white shirt and suit trousers, leaning forward over a trolley of tools.

Hal burst into a sprint, seeing what the others had not. Aksel wasn't moving.

'Aksel?' Hal reached the door and saw a small puddle of blood on the floor. He put up his hand, to prevent Hilda and Ozan from rushing forward. There was a spanner on the

228

ground, tossed down. It too had blood on it. It had been used to hit Aksel. 'Don't touch that.' He pointed at the spanner. 'It might have fingerprints on it.'

Leaning over Aksel, Hal could see his hair was matted and sticky with blood. He took a deep breath and put his fingers to the man's neck. To his intense relief, it was warm, and he could feel a pulse. 'He's alive!'

'He's badly hurt,' Hilda said. 'We must help him.'

There was a groan, and Aksel moved a little. Careful to avoid the spanner and the blood, Hilda knelt down so her face was close to his and put a hand on his arm. *'Aksel, hör mir zu. Du bist verletzt. Jemand hat dir auf den Kopf geschlagen.'*

'She's explaining that someone has hit him,' Ozan said to Hal.

Aksel gripped on to the trolley of tools, lifting his head, staring at the three children and then looking around the shed. They watched him in silence.

'Wo ist die Dampfmaschine?' His strangled whisper suggested he was in a lot of pain.

'He wants to know where the steam engine is,' Ozan said.

'Immer noch vor dem Haus, auf den Schienen,' Hilda said in a sweet reassuring voice.

'NEIN!' Aksel turned to Hal, his dark eyes wild with panic. *'Der Kessel hat kein Wasser!'* He tried to stand up, but wobbled, blinked and slumped back down.

'What's he saying?' Hal grabbed Hilda's arm. 'What's he saying?'

'He says the boiler has no water.' Hilda looked at Hal. 'What does that mean?'

'*Er wird explodieren!*' Aksel cried.

But Hal was already running back towards the house as fast as he could.

CHAPTER THIRTY

CLASS 99 BOMB

A blizzard of questions swirled through Hal's brain as he sprinted towards the house. Where was Connie? Had she hit Aksel? Why was the train still in the station? He drew in great gulps of air as he ran, choking on flakes of snow, which were falling faster now.

The steaming black locomotive was facing him as he hared through the archway, Schloss Kratzenstein towering above him. Hal threw himself across the courtyard and up the steps to the platform, running to the heavy iron coupling joint between the locomotive and the carriages, wrestling with it, trying to unhook them from the engine.

'What are you doing?' Arnie grabbed Hal from behind and wrenched him away from the train.

'Arnie! Help me!' Hal gasped. 'The boiler's got no water left. The firebox is still burning.' He pointed, and Arnie turned his head. 'We have to do something.'

Arnie stared at the locomotive. Beyond it, through the arch, he saw Ozan and Hilda, each under one of Aksel's arms,

231

trying to help the heavy man walk. He looked at Hal. 'What's happening?'

'Someone attacked Aksel,' Hal said, wriggling free from Arnie's grasp. 'He sent me. We have to get the train away from the house before it explodes.'

'Explodes?' Arnie looked stunned.

'Help me!' Hal cried out, returning to the coupling. 'There's no time!'

Arnie came to his side and together they lifted the iron bar. The tension on the buffers eased. The loco was uncoupled and Hal jumped up the ladder on to the footplate. The cabin was hot, the furnace fire roaring white and stuffed with coal. The shovel had been tossed to the ground. Hal's heart was beating fast. He looked at the dials, all with needles shuddering in red zones. The Class 99 was ancient, more than a hundred years old. The older an engine was, the more prone it was to rust and corrosion. He looked from levers to wheels, praying Aksel had replaced anything in the boiler likely to break under pressure.

'If the engine explodes,' Arnie shouted, 'it will destroy the house.' He looked up at the tower that loomed over his grandfather's room. 'Where's Opa?'

'Asleep. In bed.'

Their eyes met as they had the same thought. If the engine exploded, the tower would fall and Arnold would be killed.

'Ozan!' Arnie roared, as Hilda and her brother staggered with Aksel into the yard. '*Komm mit mir!*' And he spun round, running into the house, shouting, '*Feuer! Feuer! Raus aus dem Haus!*'

Aksel leaned against the courtyard wall so that Ozan could run after Arnie. Hilda shouted to Hal. 'Aksel says release the brake valve.'

Hal's hand went to a red lever. It was hot to the touch.

I can do this, he thought, and took the brakes off. The train slunk forward at a snail's pace.

He heard Aksel shout something in German.

'Throttle!' Hilda shouted, translating. 'Accelerate!'

Hal gulped and pushed the lever he hoped was the regulator. With a *whisht* of steam, the steam engine crawled along the tracks. His mouth was dry and his hands were shaking, but the locomotive was moving. Smoke billowed out of the chimney. Hal grabbed the rope of the bell, ringing it madly to alert people of the danger. He rang it and rang it as the engine rolled through the arch, out of the courtyard.

In the darkening twilight and swirling snow, Hal looked along the tracks and saw something that made his stomach lurch. The points at the fork in the track were set to send the engine into the train shed.

'Hilda!' he shouted, motioning to the tracks as she started running towards him. 'The points! Change the points!'

Accelerating to a sprint, Hilda passed the crawling loco, making it to the lever. She grabbed the metal bar and heaved at it, but it didn't budge.

As the engine closed in on her, Hal felt the panic in his chest bubble to boiling point. He shouted encouragement as she flung herself round to the other side of the lever, yanked up the trigger, throwing her body weight at it, pushing it with all her might. The points creaked as they shifted, clunking into place just before the iron wheels passed over the junction, taking the engine away from the train shed, towards Dead Man's Pass.

He gave Hilda a thumbs-up as he eased the regulator open a little more, praying there was enough steam in the boiler to get the little tank engine far enough away from the house.

Aksel, who was propped up against the garden wall,

holding his head with one hand, waved at him with the other. Hal waved back, and Aksel shouted, '*Spring, du Idiot! Du bringst dich noch um!*'

Hal gave him a thumbs-up. He couldn't believe it – he was doing it! He was driving the locomotive away from Schloss Kratzenstein. With every passing second, the engine moved a little further from the house and everyone in it . . . and then he had a thought that made his blood run cold. '*Herman!*' Hal exclaimed. He was in the tower. If the train exploded and brought it down, he would surely die!

Arnie and Ozan were saving Arnold. Hal looked back over his shoulder. Hilda was helping Aksel get to his feet. No one was helping Herman. Hal looked at the dials. How big was a train explosion? He didn't know how far away he had to go for Herman to be safe.

Leaning out of the cab, he looked along the track to Dead Man's Pass. If he could stop the engine in the cutting, the high rock walls might contain the explosion and protect the house. He willed the train forward, terrified to touch a lever or a dial in case it stopped the locomotive or triggered the explosion. Time seemed to slow down as Hal looked from the cab to the rails, to Dead Man's Pass. He ignored the voice in his brain that was screaming *You're driving a bomb! You're driving a bomb!*

'C'mon, Ninety-nine, you can do it,' he said, coaxing the engine along the rails, wishing it would move faster.

He poked his head out of the cab again, gauging the distance to Dead Man's Pass, and glimpsed a woman in grey, standing on the rocks. But when he looked again she was gone. He scolded himself. He knew now that the Kratzenstein curse was only a story. There was no witch. His heart was pounding so hard he felt sick. He studied the sight glass, tapping it, and the needle moved. It seemed to be saying there was a tiny bit of water left in the boiler. He looked at the levers: one of them had to be the inductor that released the water into the boiler. His hand trembled as he lowered it on to what he thought was the right one.

'*NIET!*' came a cry from above.

Hal looked up as cloaked figure dropped into the cab. He cried out, gripping the lever as he struggled, feeling himself being grabbed round his middle and hurled off the footplate, yanking the lever down.

Despite the cushion of snow, Hal hit the ground hard, but the person who had hold of him didn't let go, rolling over and over. An ear-splitting boom shook the earth beneath him, blasting all the sound and light out of the world.

CHAPTER THIRTY-ONE

BROTHERS IN ARMS

Hal lay still. His body ached, and a high-pitched noise was ringing in his ears, but as he drew in a deep breath and blinked his eyes open, he knew he was OK. He sat up carefully, finding he was wedged in a niche between boulders at the foot of a granite outcrop along from the cutting.

Steaming pieces of locomotive casing were strewn across the ground as far as he could see. The corpse of the Class 99 was buried in a landslide of rocks and boulders wedged into what was once Dead Man's Pass. A nauseating spaghetti of metal tubes snaked out and backwards, demonstrating the force of the explosion. The features of the giant skull had been blown apart.

Hal hugged his arms around himself, realizing he was lucky to be alive. The rocks around him had protected him from the blast and the debris. He thought of the figure who had grabbed him and jumped off the footplate. They seemed to have vanished. Whoever it was, they had saved his life.

Carefully testing each bit of his body, he got to his feet.

The scene looked like a battlefield. Shrapnel hung from tree branches, smoking and sizzling as it was cooled by the snow. The sky was dark, lit by a full moon, and he saw the silhouettes of bats, frightened from their haunt in the tower by the explosion.

The tower! Hal thought, spinning round, feeling giddy with relief when he saw it was still standing.

Hearing a cry, Hal made out Hilda and Ozan running across the snow towards him. Tears were streaming down Hilda's face, and she threw her arms out wide as he shuffled towards them.

'*Ich dachte du wärst tot!* I thought you were dead!' She hugged him and he winced.

'Ouch! I'm a bit bruised.' He looked at Ozan, scared of the answer to the question he had to ask. 'Is everyone OK? Is anyone hurt? The tower? Herman?'

'Yes. Everyone is OK,' Ozan said, studying Hal with awe. 'You did it.'

Hilda took his hand, leading him round to the front of the house.

Sitting on the steps up to the front door were Arnie and Herman. Herman was wrapped in his duvet, and Arnie had his arm round him. Arnold was sitting in his wheelchair, looking confused. Every window of Schloss Kratzenstein was blown in.

Aksel was slumped on a low step, and Bertha knelt beside him, holding a cloth to his injured head. Alma cried out when she saw them, pointing, and Clara burst into tears when she saw that he was alive.

Hal suddenly felt very tired. Herman was OK. The house was still standing. His legs turned to jelly, and he stumbled. But Ozan was there, putting Hal's arm over his shoulder and helping him to the steps.

'*Ist er in Ordnung?*' Alma said, coming to help. She talked with Hilda and Ozan in German. Hal was too tired to try to understand. He was sitting on the ground beside Arnold's wheelchair, and he realized he could see blue flashing lights in the distance.

'I'm sorry about your train,' Hal said, noticing that the old man was staring at it.

239

'*Nein*, Harrison.' Arnold smiled at him and pointed at the landslide of boulders on the remains of his vintage locomotive. 'You have broken the curse. *Danke schön.*'

'You know you're going to have to tell everyone the truth about the curse,' Hal said in a quiet voice, and Arnold nodded.

As the blue lights got closer, Hal saw that it was a line of vehicles. There was an ambulance and four police cars. They came up the drive and skidded to a halt in front of the house. Uncle Nat burst from one of the cars, sprinting to Hal.

'Hal! What's happened? Are you OK?'

Hilda launched into an explanation, half in English, half in German, as Uncle Nat looked from her to Hal, the buried locomotive, and back again. He looked horrified.

Then suddenly everyone was talking. Hal found himself sitting on a stretcher as a man looked into his eyes and ears with a tool that had a tiny light on it. Aksel was wheeled away to be taken to hospital. A doctor was interviewing Arnold, who was becoming more animated by the second, while Freya fussed over him. Rada came over to talk with Uncle Nat.

Clara sat down beside Herman, and Bertha sat down beside Arnie, but he didn't take his arm away from his little brother and Herman kept his head leaned against his chest.

'Ozan.' Hal called him over. 'What happened when you and Arnie went into the house?'

'We didn't know if you could move the train far enough,' Ozan replied. 'We thought the house was coming down. Arnie screamed for his mum, Clara and Alma all to get out as we ran up to Arnold's room. When we arrived, Arnie just scooped the old man up and put him in the wheelchair. Then he asked me where Herman was.' Ozan looked at the ground. 'In all the drama, I'd forgotten Herman, but Arnie didn't. I

241

told him Herman was in the tower, and Arnie told me to get his Opa out of the house and helped me get the wheelchair to the lift. Then, because I was using the lift, he ran up the stairs in the tower. Herman was asleep. Arnie wrapped him in his duvet, like a sausage, and carried him in his arms all the way down the stairs. He was coming out of the house as the train exploded. The duvet protected Herman, but Arnie was cut by flying glass.' Ozan nodded at the brothers on the step. 'They haven't moved a centimetre from each other since Bertha sat them both down so she could tend to Arnie's cuts.'

The ambulance took Aksel to the hospital, and the police spoke to Bertha at length before going into the building.

Uncle Nat sat down beside Hal.

'Are you OK?' Hal asked him.

'Not really. I'm going to be in terrible trouble when your mum finds out that you drove an exploding steam engine.'

Hal gave a weak chuckle. 'No, I mean is everything OK with the police?'

'The baron explained to them who we are.'

'It's time to tell everyone the truth,' said Hal, and Uncle Nat nodded.

CHAPTER THIRTY-TWO

BETTER TOGETHER

Clara made hot chocolate and coffee for everyone, using the servants' kitchen. The police couldn't be sure how bad the damage was to the back of the house, so the baron, Freya, Rada, Alma, Uncle Nat and Oliver followed Bertha's instructions, bringing in mattresses and bedding, turning the library into a dormitory for the night. Everyone was being kind and smiling. The brush with catastrophe had reminded them of what was important.

When the hot drinks arrived, they gathered the library chairs into a circle. Arnold wheeled forward, glancing at Hal who smiled encouragingly. Arnold cleared his throat. 'My beloved family, I will speak in English out of respect for our guests.' He nodded at Hal and Uncle Nat. 'My secrets have troubled you for long enough. It is time I told the truth.' He paused, looking at hands. 'I . . . I . . .' His eyes filled with tears.

Hal got up and went to stand beside him. 'Arnold Kratzenstein is a hero,' he said. 'Many years ago, during the Cold War, he risked his life and the family business to help bring about the reunification of Germany, by passing on information he learned about the Soviet Union.'

Everyone stared at Arnold.

'To create an air of mystery on the mountain that would help explain anything strange people might see, he invented the Kratzenstein curse. He knew the story of Gobel Babelin from the commonplace book in the library, which he'd studied because of his passion for the family business. He told the story of the man dying in the pass and spread rumours about sightings of the witch on the mountain. He boasted of the family's links to Goethe and *Faust*.' He smiled at Arnold. 'You filled your house with stuffed dead animals, kept goats and thought it funny that people were afraid of the place.' He looked at Freya, with Belladonna curled up on her lap. 'You have your father's sense of humour. You encourage people to think you're a witch because it amuses you.'

Freya chuckled. 'This is true.'

'Opa!' Arnie exclaimed. 'You made the curse up?' He was shocked. 'All those stories you told me when I was little?'

'They were just stories, Arnie. I'm sorry if . . .'

'Ha!' Arnie exclaimed in delight, looking at Herman, who was still sitting beside him. 'We're not cursed!'

'I'm not,' Herman replied with a cheeky grin, 'but you are cursed with a face like a donkey!' The brothers laughed, giddy with relief.

'Arnold did such a good job of spreading rumours that when tragedy struck and Manfred died the curse was blamed by friends and family,' Hal said.

'The curse took on a life of its own,' Arnold agreed. 'I couldn't control it.'

'Harrison Strom, how do you know so much?' Freya asked.

'He's not Harrison Strom,' Ozan said.

'You're not?' Herman looked confused.

'His name is Harrison Beck, and he's a detective,' Ozan told him.

'But he's a child.' Bertha frowned then looked at Uncle Nat. 'Who are you?'

'My name is Nathaniel Bradshaw,' Uncle Nat admitted. 'I'm Hal's uncle. We work together.' He smiled proudly at Hal.

'I invited them here, at Arnold's request,' the baron said. 'We thought it best if they pretended to be family.'

'If there's no curse, then why have all these strange things been happening?' Clara asked.

'Sir –' Hal turned to Arnold – 'do you remember the first time you saw a woman on top of Dead Man's Pass?'

'She came with the winter,' Arnold replied. 'I thought she heralded my death.'

'Did you tell anyone about her?'

Arnold shook his head.

'You said there was no witch.' Arnie frowned.

'Arnold didn't think she was a witch,' Hal said.

'I have always known that if they discovered what I did, taking government secrets across the border, it would be the end of my life,' Arnold explained.

'That is when you wrote to me,' Freya exclaimed.

'Yes,' Arnold replied. 'I wanted to make amends for the

245

lost years. I am truly sorry, *liebling*.'

'A few weeks before you saw the woman on the rocks,' Hal continued, 'did Alexander visit you with a proposal that you should sell the house and land and move to Berlin to live with him?'

Looking surprised, Arnold nodded.

'But your wife and son are buried on this mountain. You love this house. You will never leave.'

Arnold nodded. 'I wish to end my days here.'

'Alexander argued with you, and returned to Berlin. Then some weeks later Connie arrived at the house, presenting herself as a nurse who had been hired by Alexander to take care of you.'

Bertha scowled. 'Alexander did not like me looking after his father.'

'No.' Clara frowned. 'That's wrong. Alexander told me *you'd* hired Connie. He thought you were trying to control his father.'

'Nobody hired Connie,' Hal said. 'She told the people here that Alexander had hired her, and then wrote to Alexander, pretending to be Bertha, saying she'd hired a nurse called Connie to look after Arnold.'

Bertha gasped, and everybody looked shocked, including Uncle Nat.

'Rada, the letters you found in Alexander's desk – they were from a company called Stromacre?'

Rada nodded. 'They were about the purchase of the house and land for the purposes of turning the place into a health resort.'

246

'And they were signed by Nat Strom,' Hal said, 'which is why you thought Uncle Nat was behind all of the strange things that have been happening?'

'Yes, in one of the letters Nat asks Alexander if he thinks they can persuade his father to change his mind about the sale by playing on his superstitious nature and his fears regarding the family curse.'

'Not even Alexander knew that Arnold had invented the curse,' Hal said. 'It's become a part of family myth and something that even distant members know about and fear.' He smiled at Alma.

'What has this got to do with Connie?' Bertha asked.

'When we arrived, the baron introduced my uncle as Nat Strom, and Connie stared at him. That evening, she asked me why we were here. She told me to tell my dad that I wanted to go home.' He paused. 'She knew my uncle wasn't the real Nat Strom, because . . . *she is*.'

'Connie is Nat Strom?' Freya gasped.

'Natalie Strom.' Hal nodded, pulling the photograph from his pocket. 'With her heart set on buying this place, she disguised herself as Connie Müller and arrived pretending Alexander had hired her. She learned as much as she could about the curse, talking to Aksel, Arnold and Bertha. She discovered the key to the private library and read the commonplace book about the death of Frau Babelin's son.'

'It was Connie who turned the corner of the page over!' Hilda exclaimed.

'Yes. She told Aksel she'd seen the witch in the woods. She

247

frightened Arnie when he came home late one night.'

'I wasn't scared really,' Arnie muttered.

'Connie would dress up as the witch Arnold described, a ghostly face, a grey cloak, long dark hair and stand on Dead Man's Pass when she knew Arnold was playing with his trains, and likely to look out of the window.' He turned to Arnold. 'Connie thought she was scaring you with the curse. Little did she know that the description you gave out of the witch was the description of the contact you once handed over secrets to. You thought the woman you saw in the pass was an enemy agent.'

'She couldn't have been my old contact,' Arnold explained. 'My contact was the same age as me, but she had the grey cloak. I thought it was a warning.'

Hal looked around the circle of faces. 'Connie's aim was to scare Arnold, and all of you, into selling up and moving to Berlin with Alexander. If Arnold had died of a heart attack, it would have worked for her too, because the house would pass to Alexander, and he was keen to sell it.'

'All that for some land.' Clara looked stunned.

'It's not just a bit of land,' Hal said. 'You cannot buy land up here – most of it is a national park. Oliver, you told me that there's so much culture, nature and history here that tourists come from all over the world. A big hotel resort would make a lot of money, especially with its own private branch line on to the Brockenbahn.'

There was a murmur as everyone realized this was true.

'Alexander didn't know that the nurse looking after his

father was Natalie Strom. When Connie learned he was visiting, she kept out of the way, hoping her intimidation tactics would have made Arnold change his mind about the sale. But when Alexander tried again to persuade his father to sell the house Arnold refused again, and they quarrelled. Alexander was angry that his father was being so stubborn. He went to the study and drank whisky. Bertha went to talk to him about Arnie's future. Alexander had promised to create a job for him at K-Bahn, but Alexander was cross with Bertha for hiring a nurse and blamed her for his father's stubborn behaviour. They argued.' Bertha gave a slight nod of her head. 'Alexander stormed out of the house, walking down the railway line into Dead Man's Pass.'

Hal paused. Every person in the circle was holding their breath.

'What I think happened next is this: Connie had lit candles, putting them in the eyes of the skull, and was wearing the witch's grey cloak, her face painted white, ready to frighten Arnold when he looked out of his window. She must have thought it would help Alexander's case. When she sees him storming along the tracks, Connie steps out from her hiding place, forgetting her ghostly face and witch's cloak. Alexander's body is already flooded with adrenalin and whisky from the arguments he's had. The shock of the sudden appearance of the witch from the curse triggers a heart attack. Connie pulls off her wig and loosens his collar, telling him what she's doing, how she's trying to help him. Alexander grabs her face, her white make-up getting on his fingers. He's horrified by her plan to terrorize his family and his heart gives out.' He turned to the baron. 'Alexander died realizing he'd put his father's life in danger. That's why he looked the way he did.'

There was a long silence.

'But now, Connie is in trouble. Alexander is no longer able to sell her the house if Arnold dies. And she cannot run away, because that would cast suspicion on Alexander's death and her. She promotes the idea that the curse and the witch are responsible for Alexander's heart attack. She decides to stick to her plan, hoping Alexander's death will make Arnold want to sell. She must have got a nasty shock when Freya stepped off the train for the funeral and was so obviously happy to be home.'

'Because now I will inherit the house.' Freya looked at her father, and he nodded. 'I would never sell it, Papa.'

'You were here when Alexander died. I heard you say so,' Ozan said accusingly. 'Why?'

'Papa had written saying he wished us to meet. I was unsure. I brought Rada to Wernigerode. We rented a place. I hoped to pluck up the courage and knock on the door of my old home, but then came the news that Alexander had died, and I returned to Cologne.'

'But you have a plan,' Ozan persisted.

'We do,' Freya smiled at Rada. 'We're moving back here, permanently, to be close to Papa.

'Alexander's funeral was Connie's last chance to scare you all away,' Hal said. 'She increased the horror of the curse by putting blood in your gloves.'

'Where did she get it from?' Hilda wondered.

'She could have got it from a butcher in Wernigerode, or . . .'

'Oh no!' Hilda's hand went to her face. 'Not the poor goat!'

'The goat did go missing the day before the funeral,' Hal observed.

'Brutal!' Ozan grimaced.

'What about the rocks that nearly fell on us?' Herman asked. 'Did Connie do that?'

'Yes.' Hal nodded. 'Do you remember? She came to the tower and asked us what we were going to do the next day. We told her we were going into the pass for a snowball fight. The next morning, she put Arnold's boots in her bag, released the goat, and asked Aksel to help her look for it. She split off from him, put on the boots, went to the top of the pass and sent down a shower of stones and snow.'

'She attacked you?' Clara looked at Herman in horror.

'Her plan was to frighten us, and to point the finger at Aksel. He has the same shoe size as Arnold, and when we discovered the footprints in the snow he was our number one suspect.'

'And because of his locket,' Ozan said. 'It has the initials *GB* engraved on it.'

'It was Connie who told us to look out for that locket,' Hilda pointed out.

'That was his mother's necklace,' Bertha said. 'Her name was Greta Balzer before she was married.'

'At the funeral, Connie suggested Clara take Arnold back

251

to Berlin, but Arnold wouldn't hear of it. That's when she came up a new plan. She'd learned that morning, from me and Aksel, that a steam engine empty of water could explode. If the locomotive exploded in the station, the house would be destroyed. You'd have to leave. Stromacre could swoop in and buy the cursed place at a low price.'

'It would have killed Opa and Herman!' Arnie was outraged.

'Either that hadn't crossed her mind, or she didn't care,' Hal said. 'On the way back from the funeral she told Rada about the papers in Alexander's desk that incriminated Uncle Nat. She wanted you to call the police, anticipating you'd all leave the house. Having already sedated Arnold, she asked Aksel to leave the train and go with her to the train shed, where she hit him with a spanner. Returning to the loco, she filled the furnace with coal, grabbed her bags and left. Anyone searching for her would be looking for Connie Müller, not Natalie Strom.'

'I would like to get my hands on that woman,' Freya said, strangling the air in front of her.

'There's no knowing where she is now,' Hal said with a sigh.

'Well, the good news is that she isn't here any more,' Alma said. 'Now finish your drinks, children, it's bedtime. You've had a long day.'

CHAPTER THIRTY-THREE

THE RED SIGNAL

The next morning, in the library, Hal opened his eyes to see hundreds of book spines standing guard around him. Ozan and Herman were sitting on Hilda's mattress, all three of them whispering.

'You're awake!' Hilda smiled.

'We've decided,' Herman said, 'that even though you're not our cousin we'd like you to be.'

'We want to make you our honorary second cousin,' Ozan said, and the three of them nodded.

Hal beamed. 'I'd like that.'

'Do you really have to go today?' Hilda asked.

Hal nodded. 'I promised my mum I'd be home before Easter.'

'Is there time for one last snowball fight before you leave?' Ozan said.

'Definitely,' said Hal, grinning.

Clara's head peered round the library door. 'We're going to put the breakfast out here on the hall table. Collect a plate

253

and help yourself when you are ready.'

Herman bounced over to Arnie's bed and shouted, '*Aufwachen, Weichei!*' then squealed as Arnie roared like a bear and pretended to grab him.

Hal stretched and got up. Pulling on his jumper, he looked out of the library window. To his surprise, he saw a red car parked askew in the middle of the driveway. A blonde woman was struggling in the driver's seat. Standing on the bonnet of the car was a goat.

'Who's that?' asked Herman, coming to his side.

'Rufen Sie die Polizei!' Arnie shouted. 'It's Connie!'

'Oh, it's the missing goat!' Hilda did a dance of joy.

'Connie is handcuffed to the steering wheel,' said Hal, astonished.

Connie was glaring at the house and yanking her wrists against the cuffs.

'Where did she come from?' Ozan asked.

'Maybe the goat caught her.' Hilda giggled.

'Someone must have,' Arnie said, and they all turned to Hal.

'Don't look at me!' Hal said with a shrug.

The police arrived quickly and arrested Natalie Strom. Clara, Bertha and Freya wanted to give her a piece of their mind, but the baron insisted they remain inside, leaving Uncle Nat and Oliver to speak to the police. He declared that they'd been upset enough by the woman, and now must move forward and let the authorities deal with her.

As soon as the police were gone, the children ran out into the snow and began making an arsenal of snowballs. Arnie joined them, shouting, 'Brothers against the others!' beckoning Herman to his side.

Clara and Bertha sat on the steps drinking coffee and watching the children play, laughing as Arnie threw himself in front of snowballs aimed at Herman.

Uncle Nat came out with their bags and waved at Hal as a taxi came up the drive. They stopped throwing snowballs as Hal said, 'It's time for me to go.'

'Will you come and visit us in Munich sometime?' asked Hilda, and Ozan nodded.

'I'd like that.'

Herman threw his arms round Hal, and then so did Hilda and Ozan. Arnie laughed and shouted something in German before joining the hug and leaning against them with all his weight, tumbling them into the snow together, laughing.

*

Beneath the high, blue, glass arches of Berlin Hauptbahnhof, Hal and Uncle Nat alighted from their train, making their way to their next connection through the station, which was humming and bustling with travellers.

'Is it far to Brussels?' Hal asked as they studied the platform screens.

'Less than two hours after we change at Cologne,' replied Uncle Nat. 'We'll have time for a quick snack before we catch the Eurostar.' He pointed. 'Platform thirteen – that's us.'

Weaving through ambling tourists, they found space on a bench and sat down to wait for the high-speed Intercity Express train.

'Do you think Connie will go to prison for a long time?'

'I expect so.'

'She seemed so nice,' Hal said with a sigh. 'Funny how people can appear to be one way, but turn out to be someone different.' He looked at his uncle meaningfully.

'On that subject . . .' Uncle Nat said. 'I wanted to thank you for keeping my past a secret when you explained what we were doing at Schloss Kratzenstein.'

'A promise is a promise.'

'Yes, and you kept it.' Uncle Nat smiled gratefully, then glanced at the watches on his left wrist. 'We have a few minutes before the train arrives. Why don't I get us some spaghetti ice cream for the journey?'

'Spaghetti ice cream?'

'You'll love it,' said Uncle Nat. 'Back in a second.'

Hal sat with their bags, enjoying the sights and sounds of the futuristic station, when he heard a low insistent voice say, 'Don't turn round, Harrison.'

Hal froze. Out of the corner of his eye, he could see a woman with dark hair sitting on the bench directly behind

257

him. She wore a grey coat and was facing the opposite platform. He looked straight ahead, watching a harassed couple with a pushchair making their way to the lift.

'Arctic Fox?' he said quietly.

'*Da.*' There was a silence as someone passed the bench.

'Thank you.' Hal hugged his rucksack. 'Thank you for saving my life.'

'You turned on the red signal. I answered,' she said, and he noticed her unusual accent. He thought it might be Russian. 'You saved many lives.' She laughed: a low, husky sound. 'Not bad for a kid.'

'Is Arnold safe?'

'*Da.* He has nothing to worry about.'

'You're not the contact he worked with?'

'Ha! Do I sound a hundred years old to you?'

'How did you find Connie?'

'You ask a lot of questions. I have been watching Schloss Kratzenstein since the red signal was activated by the Signalman. When the nurse left the house, she did not know the tyres of her vehicle had been slashed. She did not get far.' A low chuckle. 'She telephoned for a hire car. I bring her a car, saying I am from hire car company. She got in, I cuffed her to the wheel and returned her to the house.'

Hal grinned. 'And how did you find the goat?'

'Goat? What goat?'

Hal chuckled. The goat must have found his own way home.

'I came to make sure you understand how important it is

that you keep our secret,' Arctic Fox said seriously.

'I understand,' said Hal.

'You will be known by code name: the Sleeper.'

'You can count on me.' Hal felt a thrill at being given a code name. 'What are you going to do now? Are you going back to Wernigerode?'

There was no reply. Hal waited a moment, then risked a glance behind him. The bench was empty. All he saw was a crowd of shifting strangers crossing the concourse.

'Here you are,' said Uncle Nat, returning with a tub of vanilla ice cream noodles topped with red berry sauce. 'And just in time too.' The white-and-red Intercity Express purred into the station. 'Ready for one more train journey with your boring old uncle?' he said with a twinkle in his eye.

'Always,' Hal replied with a grin. Getting to his feet, he grabbed the handle of his suitcase. 'Let's go home.'

ACKNOWLEDGEMENTS

M. G. Leonard

I would like to thank my husband, Sam Sparling, for his constant love and support, but more specifically for his drawings. He often maps out buildings and train carriages before we write them, and for this story he researched German architecture and helped create the spooky Schloss Kratzenstein.

Thank you, Sarah Hughes, our editor at Macmillan, for being a passionate reader and so understanding through the most trying of times in which to write such a complicated book to a ridiculously tight deadline. Thank you for your belief in this series, Sarah, and your patience as we try to plot our way around the world by rail. I would also like to thank Nick de Somogyi, our proof editor, for his forensic eye and enthusiasm for our rail mysteries.

This book is an incredible package and that is down to the wondrous Rachel Vale and Elisa Paganelli. I am so grateful to both these talented ladies. Elisa, each book you illustrate for us astonishes me; you capture the mood and the eye of Hal

261

so perfectly. Thank you for your extraordinary hard work and generous spirit.

I would like to thank all at Macmillan who have helped create and deliver this book into the hands of reader – one day I hope to meet you in person. Jo Hardacre, thanks for making promoting these stories an absolute pleasure.

Kirsty McLachlan, my extraordinary agent, I'm grateful as ever to have you aboard. Long may our journey continue.

Thank you, Sam Sedgman, for being a brilliant writing partner, and for taking me on my first sleeper train and all the way to the Brockenbahn. It was a fabulous adventure that I'll never forget.

And to every single book lover out there who has read and recommended our books, thank you.

Sam Sedgman

This book was written in very difficult circumstances. However, the darkest times were always illuminated by plenty of bright sparks, to whom I owe a great many thanks:

Firstly, to Maya. I will always be grateful for your friendship and support through this challenging year. Thank you for your kind heart, your words of wisdom and for being my tireless travel companion through this particularly dark adventure. I'm grateful every day that I get to call you my friend. Now, for God's sake, get some sleep.

To my parents, who have provided me with all the love in the world and plenty more besides.

To our new editor, Sarah Hughes, who boarded the footplate of this high-speed express in the middle of a snowstorm, but who has easily risen to the challenge. Despite an apparent global apocalypse, she has kept this book on timetable. Her fearsome might has no equal.

To Elisa Paganelli, Sherlock Da Vinci herself, whose illustrations work miracles, and who deserves far more praise than we can ever give her. And to Rachel Vale, whose keen eye and masterful hand has made the artwork of this book into such a brilliant package.

To the rest of the stellar team at Macmillan who have manned the signal box, oiled the points, filled the tender and done everything in their power to help our series build up a head of steam. Sam, Jo, Sarah, Alyx, Charlie and everyone else I haven't met who do so much for us without complaint: you are heroes, all.

To my agent, Kirsty McLachlan, who is as steady as the Brocken peak, and no less scary. I'm always glad you're on my team.

To my miraculous friends for supporting me through difficult times: you are too numerous to name, but you know who you are. But especially to Zoe Roberts, Kim Pearce and Roisin Symes, who have been particularly accommodating of an author in need.

To my nephew Monty, our biggest fan, who grows more like Hal every day.

To Sam Sparling, King of Calendars and Lord of Lunch.

To every bookseller, teacher and librarian who has pressed our stories into the hands of a young reader or enthusiastic grown-up – thank you from the bottom of my heart. My greatest regret of the past year is not being able to do more to visit schools and shops, to introduce myself and see your marvellous work up close. Soon, I hope, I will make amends.

And to you, dear reader, for picking up this book and coming on an adventure with us. I hope you'll stay on board for our next stop.

A NOTE FROM
THE AUTHORS

Dear Reader,

This book is inspired by real locations, railway journeys and German folklore. We would like to share some intelligence with you about the trains and the places you have encountered, and acknowledge where we have strayed from the tracks of truth.

The Night Train to Berlin

Anyone can take Hal and Uncle Nat's journey from Crewe to Wernigerode. We did most of this journey ourselves, although we started at St Pancras and took the TGV and the Nightjet sleeper, rather than the direct Trans-European Express to Berlin. Sam planned the route (with help from **seat61.com**), taking Maya on her first ever sleeper train, and sharing a compartment with a snoring Frenchwoman. There are a great many sleeper trains criss-crossing Europe, linking its beautiful cities without the need to fly. Recently there has been a

267

resurgence in the popularity of sleeper trains – with new routes opening to cities like Barcelona, Venice and Amsterdam.

The Brockenbahn

The Brockenbahn is a real railway linking Wernigerode to the Brocken peak. It is part of a narrow-gauge network criss-crossing the Harz mountains – one of the last timetabled steam railways in Europe. Our trip to the top, pulled by a Class 99 steam loco through the atmospheric pine forests and ancient rock formations, inspired this whole book.

Dead Man's Pass and the Kratzensteins

Dead Man's Pass is not real – and neither is Schloss Kratzenstein. The unusual family home is heavily inspired by Castle Wernigerode and the historic architecture of Wernigerode itself, which we recommend visiting if you get the chance.

The Kratzenstein family are named after Christian Gottlieb Kratzenstein, one of the scientists thought to have inspired Mary Shelley's *Frankenstein*.

Witches and Devils

Witches feature heavily in the folklore of the Harz mountains. Every year, on May eve, there is a festival called *Walpurgisnacht*. In legend, and in Geothe's play, *Faust,* Part I, witches fly to the peak of the Brocken to dance with the devil on *Walpurgisnacht*. Nowadays, in the villages and towns in the foothills of the

Harz mountains, people dress up as witches and devils, making bonfires and partying until dawn.

When researching for this book, we came across the story of an innocent girl who was executed at the Würzburg witch trials in Germany from 1626–1631 called Gobel Babelin. We named our character after her, because our Gobel Babelin wasn't a witch either.

Goethe

Goethe, the writer of *Faust*, is as significant in Germany as Shakespeare is in the United Kingdom.

The Cold War

There were spies in East Germany during the Cold War – and the CIA really did hide secret messages in dead rats for their agents to recover. Everything Oliver Essenbach tells Hal about the Brocken is true: it was fenced off by the Soviets and used as a listening post. When the Berlin Wall fell, and the country's two halves were reunited, the reopening of the Brocken came to be seen as a symbol of national unity.

Exploding Locomotives

Older steam engines really can explode if they run out of water – though it is rare, and other things must go wrong in order for this to be possible. The steam locomotives you see on railways today must follow strict modern safety rules to make sure this doesn't happen. No steam locomotive has exploded in the UK since 1962.

A Miniature Railway Masterpiece

Sam's Uncle David has an extensive model railway layout at his home in Somerset, which was the catalyst for creating Arnold's masterpiece at Schloss Kratzenstein. When we visited Wernigerode, we discovered a bar that delivers drinks to your table using a model train, and they tasted all the more delicious for it.

Find out more . . .

If you'd like to know more about Europe's railways, we recommend visiting one of its many railway museums – Sam visited the German Museum of Technology as research for this book and discovered that Germans invented the electric train.

Visit **adventuresontrains.com** to learn more about Hal's adventures and for videos, activities and classroom resources.

Turn the page for an exclusive peek
at Hal's next adventure,

SABOTAGE
ON THE
SOLAR
EXPRESS

<u>TRANSCRIPT OF TRIPLE ZERO[*] CALL</u>

Date of Call	11H32 29 July 202— Duration 120 seconds
Place of Call Received	Alice Springs District Police Communications Centre, Australia

ESO**: Emergency, police, fire, ambulance?

Caller: Police! No. Fire! I mean ambulance. Mate, I don't know! All three. I need all three. There's been a crash! A truck is on fire!

ESO: What's your location, sir?

Caller: I'm on the A87, Stuart Highway, north of Alice Springs.

ESO: You say there's been a crash?

Caller: There was a train . . . It went through the truck like a torpedo *(background noise, yelling)*

ESO: Is anyone injured?

Caller: Look, I don't know. I can't see. There was a truck across the rail tracks. The train didn't slow down. It smashed right through.

ESO: Is the train derailed?

Caller: No. It's still going. Heading north, towards Katherine. I saw kids onboard.

ESO: Do you mean passengers on the train?

Caller: They were up front. It looked like they're *driving* the train. But that can't be right, can it? Kids wouldn't be—
(sound of an explosion)

ESO: Hello . . .? Sir . . .? Are you all right, sir? Hello . . .?

Caller: Did you hear that? The truck exploded! *(sound of people shouting)*

ESO: Yes. Please listen. I'd like you to move a safe distance from the fire and wait for the emergency services. Will you do that for me?

Caller: Sure, but hurry up!

******** CALL TERMINATED ********

*000 is the equivalent of UK 999 or USA 911
**ESO = Emergency Services Operator

Join Hal and Uncle Nat right from the start of their
ADVENTURES ON TRAINS

'A thrilling and entertaining adventure story'
David Walliams on *The Highland Falcon Thief*

'A first-class choo-choo dunnit!'
David Solomons on *Kidnap on the California Comet*

'A high-speed train journey worth catching . . . The best yet'
The Times on *Murder on the Safari Star*

ABOUT THE AUTHORS

M. G. Leonard has made up stories since she was a girl, but back then adults called them lies or tall tales and she didn't write them down. As a grown up, her favourite things to create stories about are beetles, birds and trains. Her books have been translated into over forty languages and won many awards. She is the vice president of the insect charity Buglife, and a founding author of Authors4Oceans. She lives in Brighton with her husband, two sons, a fat cat called Kasper, a dog called Nell, and a variety of exotic beetles.

Sam Sedgman is a bestselling novelist, playwright and award-winning digital producer. His work has been performed internationally and shortlisted for the Courtyard Theatre Award. Written with his friend, M. G. Leonard, *The Highland Falcon Thief* was Sam's first book for children. A lifelong mystery enthusiast, he grew up with a railway at the bottom of his garden and has been mad about trains ever since. He lives in London.

Elisa Paganelli was born in Italy and since childhood hasn't been able to resist the smell of paper and pencils. She graduated from the European Institute of Design in Turin and worked in advertising, as well as running an award-winning design shop and studio. She now collaborates as a freelance designer with publishers and advertising agencies all over the world, including designing and illustrating *The House With Chicken Legs* (Usborne) and the Travels of Ermine series (Usborne).

Coming soon

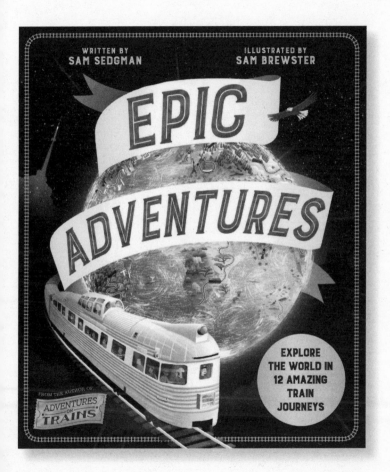